I0686841

Pulpit Science Fiction

George L. Murphy

CSS Publishing Company, Inc., Lima, Ohio

PULPIT SCIENCE FICTION

Library of Congress Cataloging-in-Publication Data

Murphy, George L., 1942-
  Pulpit science fiction / George L. Murphy.
    p. cm.
  ISBN 0-7880-2377-2 (perfect bound : alk. paper)
  1. Story sermons. 2. Bible—Sermons. 3. Science fiction—Religious aspects—
Christianity. 4. Sermons, American—21st century. 5. Episcopal Church—Sermons. I.
Title.

BV4307.S7M87 2005
252—dc22

                                                            2005015001

For more information about CSS Publishing Company resources, visit our website at
www.csspub.com or e-mail us at custserv@csspub.com or call (800) 241-4056.

Cover design by Jay Cookingham
ISBN 0-7880-2377-2   PRINTED IN U.S.A.

For Dona, Anastasia, and Katherine,
who watched Star Trek *with me*
and asked me not to
criticize its science

Table Of Contents

Introduction

The function of preaching is to communicate God's Law and — pre-eminently — the gospel of Jesus Christ. It is to be proclamation of God's Word, a living word which is "like fire ... and like a hammer that breaks a rock in pieces" (Jeremiah 23:29). Preaching is to be a means by which the living Christ encounters people. If it really is that, then it may have many different styles and techniques, but it should never be boring.

In one sense, the fundamental sermonic form is the proclamation of God's Word as *news*: "The kingdom of God is at hand." "Jesus Christ is risen." "Your sins are forgiven." Such *kerygmatic* preaching is more than simply the communication of information. "Gospel" or "evangel" means good *news*. There is also a need to explain the implications of this news, and thus for teaching, or *didactic* preaching.

Traditional preaching has usually had one or the other of those forms, or a combination of them. But there is another form that goes back to the Bible itself — the story. Parables were one of Jesus' favorite ways of communicating the truth of the kingdom of God to his audiences, and in recent years there has been renewed interest in story sermons. Richard A. Jensen's book, *Telling the Story: Variety and Imagination in Preaching*, sets out these three homiletic forms and provides examples of each type. Story sermons are not expositions of the biblical text, but they should intend to express the theme of the text in story form.[1]

In spite of this renewed interest in story sermons, there is one type of story that hasn't been used very much in preaching: the science fiction story. The purpose of this book is to make a small contribution toward remedying that situation.

Even though I grew up in the church, I learned to like science fiction before I really appreciated sermons. That's not because I was uninterested in the Christian faith or because the preaching that I heard growing up was bad, but let's face it: A lot of traditional preaching doesn't have the excitement that stories of space exploration, time travel, or telepathy do. Sermons are generally pitched at an adult level, and it takes a certain amount of maturity to understand and appreciate them.

When I first started reading science fiction in the mid-1950s, it was often thought of as a genre directed to teenage boys and adults who hadn't quite grown up yet. But that was also about the time that science fiction began to be accepted as legitimate adult literature. Well-financed films (as distinguished from the old Grade-B space operas) like *Forbidden Planet, 2001: A Space Odyssey*, and *Star Wars*, and television series such as *Star Trek* have made science fiction mainstream. A lot of people who wouldn't consider themselves fans of science fiction, have some familiarity with it. Thus, it seems to be a form that can, in moderation, be useful for preaching.

With a couple of exceptions, all the sermons here have actually been preached at least once. They are not expositions of biblical texts, but each one tries to bring out in story form some aspect of a biblical passage. (They are arranged in the traditional order of the biblical texts on which they are based.) I have, of course, done some updating and tinkering with them to some degree for publication, and have also provided some comments on each one. I've also included among the sermons one *non*-story effort, the second in the collection. This is a kerygmatic sermon that uses a popular film with a science fiction element as an illustration.

An appendix includes an earlier essay of mine on religion and science fiction, as well as an internet preaching resource that I wrote the week that the film, *The Matrix Reloaded*, was released. While that has of course lost its immediate relevance, I hope that some of the reflections on preaching which makes contact with popular science fiction will be helpful.

Those who have done much story preaching have probably "borrowed" some of their stories from some other sources. Writing a story sermon is, in my experience, generally harder than developing one of the kerygmatic or didactic type, and once a story has been developed and found successful, it seems a shame just to put it in the proverbial barrel and never use it again. In publishing this collection, I expect that the stories here will be used, perhaps with modifications, by other preachers. But I hope that this work will also encourage other clergy to become more familiar with science fiction and the crafting of story sermons, and to develop science fiction story sermons of their own.

I am grateful to members of my previous congregation, St. Mark Lutheran Church in Tallmadge, Ohio, and to those of the parish where I am presently on staff, St. Paul's Episcopal Church in Akron, Ohio, for hearing and responding to some of these homilies over the years. I also want to express my thanks to my wife, Dona, who has read many of these sermons, made suggestions for their improvement, and encouraged me to develop this style of preaching.

1. Richard A. Jensen, *Telling the Story: Variety and Imagination in Preaching* (Minneapolis: Augsburg Press, 1980).

Chapter One

Improving The Species

Genesis 6:1-4

*When people began to multiply on the face of the
ground, and daughters were born to them, the sons of
God saw that they were fair; and they took wives for
themselves of all that they chose. Then the LORD said,
"My spirit shall not abide in mortals forever, for they
are flesh; their days shall be one hundred twenty
years." The Nephilim were on the earth in those days
— and also afterward — when the sons of God went in
to the daughters of humans, who bore children to them.
These were the heroes that were of old, warriors of
renown.*   — Genesis 6:1-4

Pieces of ancient myth — the gods who lusted after human
women, begetting half-divine superheroes. This broken myth is
used by the biblical writer to speak about the sinfulness and corruption of humanity, and to oppose the idea that divinity can be
propagated biologically. But perhaps we can use it to speak about
a modern way of looking at humanity which has been called "the
gene myth," the belief that we are completely determined by our
genes. Perhaps.

*   *   *   *   *

The godlike beings came to earth when humanity was young
and new at the business of intelligence and having dominion. The
species was still a lot like its primate cousins, and the gods — we
would call them aliens or extraterrestrials today — circled the earth
in their starship. They sent down "away-teams" and, carefully hidden, observed a species in a state of development much like that
of their own race a million years before. The humans were very
primitive, just beginning to show real skill in making stone tools.

11

There was plenty of fighting between little isolated groups. But they had started to use their brains, and there were some signs of cooperation among them.

The gods were intrigued, for intelligence is rare in the galaxy. They saw the potential this new species had and they knew their own potential, their expertise in analyzing and engineering life at the molecular level. It was an ability they had perfected for millennia and had used to develop new crops and animals on their home planet. They had eliminated defects in their own species and had established genetically clean colonies in several planetary systems. A great deal of good had been accomplished, and now they had a new opportunity.

The gods considered themselves to be a highly moral species. They believed in a Supreme Being who had given them the task of improving the world. So as the captain and the heads of the various scientific departments sat in the captain's ready room and watched the videos of this species they had found at its dawning, and examined the reports of the away-teams, it was quite natural for the chief of molecular biology to say finally, "We can help them."

"What do you propose?" asked the captain. "Give them some of our technology?"

"No need for that," answered the scientist. "They'll develop their own technologies. But we can ensure that those technologies will be used for good. We can improve these people ourselves. They can be spared the thousands of years of struggle and all the mistakes our ancestors had to make."

When the plan was set out, all the officers were soon in agreement. What better way to help this species than to give them some of the properties of their own advanced race? If, as they believed, life was determined by genes, then genetic improvement was absolute improvement.

It was a straightforward matter for them to translate their own genetic coding to that of terrestrial species. They secretly abducted a number of the humans (of course doing them no harm — and it was for a good cause). They altered the DNA in the somatic cells of humans and made use of their well-established cloning techniques to impregnate the daughters of humans. After ensuring safe births of healthy offspring, they released mothers and children back into optimum habitats.

The gods secretly observed the growth of their children, for they thought of these beings as if they were their own. They tested them periodically to be certain that the intended physical and mental enhancements had resulted. The children were much more intelligent, quicker, and stronger than unaltered humans. After several years, the gods were sure that their offspring would survive and prosper, so their starship left earth orbit to return to their home system.

Three generations passed for the gods. Another starship came into the solar system, and the sons of the gods came back to the earth to view their handiwork. The earth had orbited the sun many times, but on an evolutionary timescale it had been only a little while since their intervention. They expected, however, to see measurable improvement in the species that they had helped with their advanced molecular technology.

Humanity had indeed changed, and the earth had changed. High resolution scans showed gatherings of dwellings and what might be the beginnings of agriculture. Progress had been made. But when an away-team returned from its mission, the news it brought was unsettling. "There is extreme social stratification and excessive violence among these humans," the team leader reported to the assembled officers.

"Of course there's violence and role differentiation," said one of the scientists. "That's part of evolution. Nobody expected that all to be eliminated. But surely the enhanced intelligence of leaders is helping them to overcome those tendencies."

"I'm afraid not," said the team leader. "Now greater intelligence seems to give violence and domination greater scope. They have designed new weapons. Those who already have the necessities of life organize campaigns of conquest against other tribes. They have developed concepts of private property, and the stronger are able to own the weaker."

"But this is impossible," burst out the chief geneticist. "Our predecessors knew what they were doing. They didn't design these humans to be vicious slave owners."

"Perhaps there were errors in translating the genetic codes," offered a computer scientist. "Some mistakes may have been made. We need to analyze the data again and get it right."

Debate among the scientists went on for several minutes until the captain signaled them to silence. They looked at their commander expectantly.

"Maybe," said the captain, "there is a more fundamental problem. Is it possible that the achievement of a peaceful and just society requires more than genetic health? Perhaps — and I know that this goes against everything we've believed for generations — perhaps we are not determined entirely by our genetic makeup."

There were gasps from around the room. "But how...?" "What else...?"

"I disagree completely," said an engineer. "What we need to do is to figure out the mistakes our predecessors made and go down and correct them. Get these humans developing in the right direction."

"No," said the captain. "The mistake our predecessors made was to overestimate their understanding of themselves, and to think that they could apply their limited knowledge to decide the fate of another species. What we did was just a more sophisticated version of what we've seen going on down on this planet — the use of superior knowledge and technology to determine the lives of other intelligent beings. Our predecessors meant well. Let that be their memorial."

"But with no further intervention, what will happen to these humans?" demanded a sociologist.

"They are still intelligent beings, and evolution goes on. The course of their development may change," said the captain, "but we will not intervene further. Any help for them must come from another quarter."

Comment

For some time I had thought that a story sermon on genetic engineering or cloning might be based on this text from Genesis 6, but there were a couple of problems — besides that of developing the sermon itself — involved with this. The text does not occur in the lectionary for Sundays and festivals, and there is no natural occasion when it could be used in a congregation. In addition, the idea of contacts between early humans and extraterrestrials has been heavily compromised by irresponsible speculations, including the notion that this text might be a report of such encounters. [See, for example, Erich Von Däniken, *Chariots of the Gods* (New York: Bantam, 1968).] The Raelian cult with its emphasis on cloning is of particular concern in this regard. I did not want to give people who had little scientific knowledge the idea that there was any factual basis for these claims. (For serious discussion of anything that might be considered evidence for "ancient astronauts" see Carl Sagan and I. S. Shklovskii, *Intelligent Life in the Universe* [San Francisco: Holden-Day, 1966], ch. 33.)

Then I was invited to be the worship leader for the October 2000 Consultation on Human Cloning convened in Chicago by the Department of Studies of the Evangelical Lutheran Church in America. At the Sunday Eucharist, there was an opportunity to preach to this small group of specialists that was focusing on issues related to cloning, and a story sermon seemed to be a good way to complement the discussions that were going on. I am thankful to the Department of Studies for permission to reprint the sermon from the published papers of the consultation, *Human Cloning: Papers from a Church Consultation* (Chicago Department of Studies of the Evangelical Lutheran Church in America, 2001), edited by Roger A. Willer.

The term "broken myth" in the introductory paragraph is taken from Brevard S. Childs' book, *Myth and Reality in the Old Testament* (Naperville, Illinois: Alec R. Allenson, 1960), where Genesis 6:1-4 is discussed on pages 49-57. The phrase "the gene myth" is due to Ted Peters', *Playing God* (New York: Routledge, 1997).

A note on the Genesis text may be helpful. In verse 3 of the New Revised Standard Version, which I generally use for public reading, has God say, "My spirit shall not abide in mortals forever." In the interest of inclusive language this version often used "mortal" for "human being," as it does here in rendering the Hebrew *ádham*, but this is a poor choice. Here it reduces God's statement to a tautology, for the point is precisely that human beings

15

will not be immortal. (A similar problem occurs in Revelation 21:3-4, where in the NRSV, "See, the home of God is among mortals" is followed by the statement that "Death will be no more.") Thus "humans" or "human beings" would be better inclusive translations, but I leave it to other preachers to decide what version to use.

Chapter Two

Signs And The Sign

Exodus 14:19-31

Signs was one of summer 2002's hit movies. Mel Gibson stars as a priest who has left the ministry after an accident in which his wife was killed, an event that seems to have destroyed his faith. He's living with his two small children and his brother on a farm. Then circles and other strange markings begin to appear in his cornfield.

The film doesn't have to explain about these circles because they've been in the news off and on in the real world since they started appearing in England in the '80s. Some people think that they're the result of UFO landings or something of the sort, but for the past ten years they've been considered a hoax since a couple of Englishmen demonstrated how they made the circles, themselves.

Still, believers continue to think that the circles were made by aliens, because — well, because for one reason a lot of people feel very lonely in this huge, ancient, expanding universe that science has disclosed to us. It's hard for them to believe in traditional religion in this context, but terrible to think that we're all alone in emptiness. It would be comforting to know that there were other intelligent species in the universe — perhaps even if they were hostile.

So we think we know what's going on in the film when the crop circles appear, and television begins to show mysterious saucer-like lights hovering over the world's cities. The crop markings are indeed signs, landing markers for an alien invasion.

But this isn't just one more *War of the Worlds* or *Independence Day*. There are other signs, more subtle signs — or coincidences, if you insist, and we realize that the real crisis is not just another threat to people's lives. Cancer or gunshot can kill you as effectively as a hostile alien. The real crisis is what has happened, and what will happen, to the priest's faith. And in the end — well, that's why you should see the movie.

In our reading from Exodus, a strong east wind drives the sea back and makes a path for the Hebrew slaves to escape from the Egyptian army. It was a sign of God's favor, the Lord's way of liberating his people. Or was it? Perhaps it was just a coincidental timing of the weather. Maybe Israel was just lucky.

People often look for signs to show them what to believe or what to do, or how to get what they need. "If only God would give me a sign!" And sometimes we get signs we didn't ask for, or even want.

For us, for whom those images of the Twin Towers crashing to the ground are still vivid — was that a sign of divine wrath or of something else? Are there any signs of hope in today's world or are we on our own, left to work things out among ourselves?

The problem is that signs are usually ambiguous, and we can read what we want into them. There's an old story of a farmer who had been asking God for a sign to tell him what he should be doing with his life. One morning he looked up in the sky and saw clouds forming perfect letters "PC." "Preach Christ!" he exclaimed. "That's what God wants me to do." And he was all set to sell the farm and go into the ministry until one of his neighbors pointed out that the letters "PC" could just as well mean "Plant corn."

It's not surprising that signs seem ambiguous. A sign can bring someone to faith — but only if that person is in some sense open to faith. If you think you already know the answer, you won't let a sign point you anywhere else.

The Bible is full of signs, and of people asking for them. In the Gospel of John, all the miraculous things that Jesus does — turning water into wine, raising Lazarus from the dead, and all the rest, are called "signs." "Jesus did this, the first of his signs, in Cana of Galilee, and revealed his glory; and his disciples believed in him." It sounds like a dream come true for the people who say, "If only God would give me a sign!" But it doesn't seem to work that way. At the end of Jesus' ministry we're told of the crowds that "although he had performed so many signs in their presence, they did not believe in him."

And those who demand that Jesus give them a sign from heaven get a blunt answer. "An evil and adulterous generation asks for a sign, but no sign will be given to it." No sign, that is, "except the sign of the prophet Jonah. For just as Jonah was three days and three nights in the belly of the sea monster, so for three days and three nights the Son of Man will be in the heart of the earth." The only sign you will get is Christ in the tomb.

Speeches at graduations are usually pretty forgettable, but I remember vividly one line from the address at my seminary graduation: "At some points in your ministry you will ask God for a sign, and the only sign you will get is the sign of Jonah." It's something of which we all need to be reminded. What we get is the sign of death and resurrection, out of slavery into freedom, through the sea to the promised land.

That is a sign of hope, and not just because of the possibility of resurrection. We grab hold of the idea of resurrection too quickly anyway. The sign of Jonah is first of all the sign of death, of the Son of Man in the heart of the earth. It points to the truth that God has come into our world to share in our human condition, in the evils that our sin brings upon us, in our suffering and our dying. There is a good reason why the fundamental sign that marks Christian churches, the sign that we use most in worship, is the cross. It is a sign that points us to the true cross upon which the Son of God died, and it reminds us of his words to us that we must be prepared to take up our crosses and follow him.

The cross points us to the reality of God. People often talk rather glibly about God — God wills this or that, God rewards or punishes, and so forth. "I can't believe a God would allow that" they say when some disaster happens. "If only God would give me a sign." But what God are we talking about?

The Christian claim is that God is made known in the death and resurrection of Christ, so that the cross is the sign of God. If you want to know where God is at work, look first for that sign, for the crosslike events of the world. "The Son of God was crucified for all and for everything," Saint Irenaeus said, "having traced the sign of the cross on all things." God is active in the world, in solidarity with those who fail and suffer and die, so that none of their pains need be without hope.

In the light of the cross, we read our text from Exodus and see in the blast of the east wind the work of God bringing his people out of slavery to freedom. In the light of the cross, we look back at the events of September eleventh and see — well, we're probably still too close to that to read it very well. But it was surely not just the wrath of a vindictive deity, or the triumph of evil, or a guarantee of a trouble-free life. God is active for life in the presence of destruction.

In your own life, don't look just for the easy or obvious answers. Learn from the story of Jesus, from the whole of scripture, who God is. Then you will be better able to discern God's will for you, and bear in mind that often a sign of God's will is that you are led where you did not plan to go.

In order to read the signs, you have to keep your eyes and mind and heart open. And you have to look at things in the light that God gives.

Comment

As I noted in the Introduction, this is not a science fiction story sermon but one that refers to a science fiction film. *Signs*, starring Mel Gibson, was one of the popular movies in the summer of 2002, and this sermon was preached in September of that year. The film used science fiction to convey a religious theme: The way in which Gibson's character, the priest, returns to pastoral ministry (after, we assume, recovery of his faith), and not merely the appearance of extraterrestrials, is what the movie is really about. In light of Gibson's later efforts to present *The Passion Of The Christ*, this religious emphasis is not surprising.

I hope that this sermon gives some idea of how a preacher can use a currently popular science fiction film as an illustration in a more or less traditional homiletic format. Some — perhaps most — of the people in the congregation won't have seen the movie in question, and the preacher has to give at least a sketch of the plot. But, as in this case, it isn't necessary to give away everything. Leaving "how it turns out" unstated may encourage some who haven't been to the movie to see it, and then perhaps reflect back on the sermon.

Biblical texts quoted here are from John 2:11; 12:37; and Matthew 12:39-40. The statement by Irenaeus is from *On the Apostolic Preaching*, and was quoted in this form by P. Evdokimov in *Scottish Journal of Theology* 18.1, 1965, p. 5.

Chapter Three

The Promised Land

Deuteronomy 34:1-12

Moses had been quite a mountain climber in his day. He was very old now but he was still pretty strong, and his wind was good. Sometimes in the evenings he would think back to all those climbs — like the first time he had gone up Sinai, and seen the bush that burned but was not burned up, and heard God's call. Sinai — boy, he had sure climbed *that* mountain often enough when God was giving the Law to Israel! Up and down, up and down, sometimes carrying heavy stone tablets. And on top of Sinai he had had the vision of heaven which was the pattern for the tabernacle.

There had been other climbs — mountains to go up so that he could pick out a route, or choose a site for battle. And Mount Hor — he and his brother, Aaron, the priest, had had to climb that mountain when it was time for Aaron to die. That had been hard, for both of them knew what lay at the top. It would be the place for the priest to lay aside his sacred vestments and then to lay down his life.

Yes, there had been a lot of mountains in Moses' life. But now he was 120 years old and had led the people of Israel to the border of the promised land, to the River Jordan. The job was over. God had told Moses that he wouldn't be allowed to enter the land of Canaan. Moses knew that he hadn't been perfect, and though it was a disappointment, he supposed that it was fair. God didn't *owe* him anything, after all. Besides, God had promised to send another prophet like Moses someday, to lead Israel, so that the people would continue to have God's guidance.

And as the old man was thinking about all this, God said, "Moses!" And as always, Moses answered, "Here I am."

"Moses, I want you to climb Mount Nebo."

"Another mountain? At my age?" But Moses followed orders. Early in the morning he started on his way, carrying just some water and a little bread, and toiled up the rocky slopes all day. It was hard, dry work. Finally, in the late afternoon, he stood at the top of Nebo and looked toward the west.

It was a magnificent view. Moses saw the land of promise — *all* the land that God had spoken of to Abraham and Isaac and Jacob. It was a beautiful land, stretching from the southern desert to snow-capped Hermon in the far north. God had often told him about it so that he could encourage the people with a picture of their goal. "A good land, a land with flowing streams, with springs and underground waters welling up in valleys and hills, a land of wheat and barley, of vines and fig trees and pomegranates, a land of olive trees and honey." Finally, Moses was seeing it. He almost asked God to change his mind about letting him go over into it.

Instead, he peered into the distance. Moses was a seer, and no matter how old he had become, "his sight was unimpaired." His prophetic vision pierced through matter to the Great Sea in the west. His sight was released from the common sense bounds of space-time and probed the future. He saw the bands of Israelites cross Jordan with his successor Joshua at their head. He saw their journey end, saw them take possession of the land and Joshua standing on Mount Gerizim to repeat the Law of God to them.

He looked farther, and on top of Mount Zion saw the glorious Temple built. He saw God's chosen king there, reigning over the land.

And farther still, he looked into the years and centuries and saw a light shining from the north, on Mount Tabor. Moses himself stood there, revealed to his own sight with the Prophet Elijah, speaking with Jesus the Messiah about "his exodus, which he was about to accomplish at Jerusalem." The scene was bathed in the uncreated light of God shining from the Messiah. God had shielded Moses from the full blinding glare of that light on Sinai but he had caught a glimpse of it. He had a shock of recognition then. The one who shone like the sun wasn't just prophet and king. This was the one who spoke to Moses from the burning bush and gave the Law on Sinai.

And by that light, Moses saw a mountain that he might otherwise have missed. It could hardly even be called a mountain — it was barely a hill, just a big rock. But Moses saw with no ordinary sight. He saw the agony and bloody sweat and scourging. And the lawgiver, who had proclaimed that "anyone hung on a tree is under God's curse," saw the God of Israel hanging forsaken on the cross.

He saw the blood and darkness, and the sharpened ears of the prophet caught the groans of the dying thieves and the rumbling of the earthquake and a voice saying, "As Moses lifted up the serpent in the wilderness, so must the Son of Man be lifted up." He saw the one who lives forever and ever, die.

Moses saw the little hill of Golgotha stretched toward the sky. It was a stairway reaching from earth to heaven like the one Father Jacob had seen in his dream. He saw the people of Israel passing through the sea, the waters of death walled on their right hand and on their left, chanting, "I will sing to the LORD, for he has triumphed gloriously; horse and rider he has thrown into the sea."

He saw *all* the nations pass up the shining stairway of the cross, out of slavery into the freedom of the promised land, singing to God in every language of the world: "The glorious company of apostles praise you. The noble fellowship of prophets praise you. The white-robed army of martyrs praise you. Throughout the world the holy Church acclaims you."

All of the people of God crossing over Jordan into the promised land, into God's eternal hope and glory.

And Moses said to God, "May I cross over into the promised land?"

And God said, "All right."

And Moses died.

Comment

The idea that Moses, as a prophet (Deuteronomy 34:10), could "see through time" is what gives this a science fiction quality. The story is intended to show the broad sweep of salvation history and the biblical flavor of it is, I hope, enhanced by weaving into it a number of biblical quotations. The biblical texts are from, respectively, Deuteronomy 8:7-8 and 34:7; Luke 9:31 (but with "exodus" rather than NRSV's "departure" as a literal rendering of the

Greek *exodon*); Deuteronomy 21:23; John 3:14; and Exodus 15:1. The final quotation is from the *Te Deum* (in the version of the International Consultation on English Texts used in, the *Lutheran Book of Worship* and others). Of course, mention of where these texts come from should not be pedantically included in the sermon itself!

The account of Moses' death is the Old Testament reading for Transfiguration Sunday of Year C in the *Lutheran Book of Worship*'s lectionary and provided there is a good transition from the Epiphany season to Lent. This text was displaced in favor of Exodus 34:29-35 in the Revised Common Lectionary, presumably because of the reference to this account of the shining of Moses' face in the Second Lesson, 2 Corinthians 3:12—4:2, but the preacher ought to have some freedom to adjust such matters.

Chapter Four

The Great Physician

Isaiah 52:13—53:5

It's the first day for the new doctor at a rundown hospital, an institution that always has a lot of charity cases and is chronically short of money. The doctor who is coming has been preceded by a great reputation for being able to deal with a wide range of difficult cases. He has credentials from a first-rate school, a spectacular residency, several influential publications — all the credentials a doctor could want. The people at the hospital are surprised that they were able to get him.

There are some on the staff who are skeptical and even jealous. "We don't need some high-powered academic," they've been saying. "We've got to have somebody who can handle the day-to-day routine here, not a *wannabe* Albert Schweitzer, slumming. We'll see pretty quickly how he deals with the real world!" But today they're being polite and keeping quiet about their doubts.

The new doctor is William Jones — not a spectacular name. But when you keep his record in mind and then see him in the flesh, it seems almost too good to be true. He reminds you of one of the television doctors like Dr. Kildare or Peter Benton. Dressed in a well-tailored expensive suit, he's handsome and confident, exuding an air of care and competence.

There are introductions, a quick look at his new office, and then Dr. Jones wants to get right to work. One of the skeptics says, "I'm sure you'll want to see some of our difficult cases. And the ER — we're understaffed there and we always have a lot of stabbing and gunshot cases coming in."

"We'll get there," Dr. Jones replies.

On their way through the halls they see overworked professionals hurrying on their rounds. They are near the waiting room for the Intensive Care Unit, where the patients with the most serious problems lie. Family members are keeping vigil. One old

27

woman sits slumped over in a chair, weary and red eyed, twisting her purse in her hands. She's known that her husband is going to die soon, but it's so hard to give him up after nearly sixty years together.

Suddenly Doctor Jones stops and waves the other doctors and nurses and administrators back. He kneels next to the old woman and speaks quietly for a minute. He holds her hand, listens to her, and then says a few more words and she smiles at him. "Yes, I'm sure I'll be all right," she says. "I do need to rest. Thank you for talking to me." She is no longer crying.

The doctor gently disengages his hand and moves on with the others. As the nurses and other doctors explain procedures and point out problems, he continues to ask sharp questions. But they notice that he seems subdued and rather tired. His voice breaks once or twice, almost as if he were crying.

The group enters a unit with a number of AIDS patients. Several of the doctors glance at one another. These are sophisticated health care professionals with a lot of experience, and have gotten past their initial reactions to this disease, but in the back of their minds they remember that most of these people — the sexually promiscuous, the drug users, the prostitutes — are here because of their own actions. And, there is a more biting truth for doctors who are measured by their abilities to heal and keep people alive. Their advanced scientific knowledge can't really help these AIDS victims. Their patients are going to die, and doctors feel that they're failures when that happens.

Doctor Jones stops at the bed of a haggard young woman who has pneumonia and is gasping for breath. Her skin is blotchy and discolored with the ugly Kaposi's sarcoma that is typical of the disease. He glances at her chart — IV drugs, prostitution — doubly dangerous and doubly foolish. She doesn't have long to live.

The doctor again waves the others away. He sits at her bedside and, not stopping to put on rubber gloves, holds her hand and talks softly with her. He listens to her complain, for the hundredth time and with a great deal of truth, about being used by other people. He checks her chart again, makes a few notes, and suggests some changes in treatment to another doctor for whom he's motioned.

He gets up slowly as if he were tired, coughing a bit. He is not quite to the door when the woman suddenly sits up. "Are you feeling better?" asks a nurse.

"I *am* better!" she cries. "He healed me!" And amazingly, she does look healed. The other AIDS patients look at Doctor Jones with wonder and begin reaching out to try to touch him. But now he is wheezing loudly as he breathes. He looks old, and his elegant suit seems too big. At his wrists and beneath his loose collar can be seen purplish blotches.

They get out into the hall but the other professionals are concerned — not just for him but for patients. His hands are trembling and he couldn't start an IV, let alone perform any major procedure. One of the skeptics mutters to another, "He'd better get back to his desk. Our patients are hard on the boy wonder."

He stops at the door of a room. Inside is an old man who is unconscious and beyond hope of recovery. His heart and lungs are still working, but his life is just a formality, now. Doctor Jones glances at the name on the door and walks into the room, up to the bedside. "John," he says in a weary voice. He leans on the side of the bed for support. "John," he says again. "Get up!"

Now the skeptics speak openly. "This is crazy! Does he think he's a miracle worker? We've got to get him out of here. He's falling apart." But the doctor repeats, "John — Get up!" And John sits up and smiles. "Hi, Doc," he says. "Am I going home today?"

The doctor doesn't answer. He has collapsed on the floor. The nurses and doctors rush to him and see that his breathing has stopped. When they roll him over on his back they hardly recognize the handsome, confident young doctor. If he weren't wearing the same suit, which is now sagging all over the scrawny body, they wouldn't know that it was the man who had walked confidently into the hospital an hour ago. There is nothing handsome about him anymore. His eyes are red from weeping, his skin is discolored, and there is a trickle of blood from his mouth. He lies there disfigured and still.

One of the other doctors kneels beside him to check his pulse and breathing, and then looks up and says, "He's dead."

"But he healed those people."

"What should we do? What can we do?"
"*We* can't do anything."

See, my servant shall prosper; he shall be exalted and lifted up, and shall be very high. Just as there were many who were astonished at him — so marred was his appearance, beyond human semblance, and his form beyond that of mortals — so he shall startle many nations; kings shall shut their mouths because of him; for that which had not been told them they shall see, and that which they had not heard they shall contemplate.

Who has believed what we have heard? And to whom has the arm of the LORD been revealed? For he grew up before him like a young plant, and like a root out of dry ground; he had no form or majesty that we should look at him, nothing in his appearance that we should desire him. He was despised and rejected by others; a man of suffering and acquainted with infirmity; and as one from whom others hide their faces he was despised and we held him of no account.

Surely he has borne our infirmities and carried our diseases; yet we accounted him stricken, struck down by God, and afflicted. But he was wounded for our transgressions, crushed for our iniquities; upon him was the punishment that made us whole, and by his bruises we are healed. — Isaiah 52:13—53:5

Comment

The fourth Servant Song of Isaiah is a traditional reading for Good Friday. The healing in this story can be understood either as a metaphor for salvation from sin, as it often is, or as the actual healing of physical and mental ills. The two are closely related: The Greek *sozo* in the New Testament can refer both to spiritual salvation and to physical healing, and in "salvation" in the fullest sense the two go together.

Part of the text from Isaiah, "He took our infirmities and bore our diseases," is quoted in Matthew 8:17 at the end of a series of stories about Jesus' healings of the sick. Dietrich Bonhoeffer saw this as a key to understanding all the work of the God revealed in Christ.

> *God lets himself be pushed out of the world on to the cross. He is weak and powerless in the world, and that is precisely the way, the only way, in which he is with us and helps us. Matthew 8:17 makes it quite clear that Christ helps us, not by virtue of his omnipotence, but by virtue of his weakness and suffering.*[1]

In this case, I think that it is probably more effective to read the text after the sermon rather than in its traditional position at the beginning.

This sermon was first preached on Good Friday of 1988, at a time when the prospect of any successful treatment for AIDS seemed very remote, so that the disease was even more of a stigma than it is today. Treatments have been developed in the intervening years, but I've chosen to keep the image quite grim. Other preachers might want to adapt this, and perhaps use other physical or mental ailments, in accord with the needs and concerns of their congregations.

---

1. Dietrich Bonhoeffer, *Letters and Papers from Prison*, enlarged edition (New York: Macmillan, 1972), pp. 360-361.

Chapter Five

Exiles

Ezekiel 34:1 1-16, 20-24

Our story takes place on a small green-blue planet, partly covered with clouds, which circles near the warmth of a medium-sized yellow star. No, this is not the earth circling the sun. The earth is very different now. Its oceans are still blue but the land is gray, covered with radioactive dust. In the final throes of the environmental crisis of the late twenty-first century, when nations were fighting desperately for the last of the oil and clean water and other resources, nuclear weapons were finally used. Those old predictions about nuclear winter turned out to be right. Within a few weeks it was all over. There are still bacteria and there is a little life in the oceans, but very few things move on the planet's surface.

That happened just a few years after the first ships were sent out beyond the solar system. They weren't "starships" like those in the old science fiction movies, zipping around the galaxy in a matter of days. They were huge lumbering arks that would take generations to creep across the tremendous distances between the stars. With carefully controlled reproduction and use of resources, there was just a chance that one or two ships might find planets where human beings could live. It had been an act of desperation, a wild gamble, to send them out. But those who had done it, who had used earth's last precious resources to launch the ships knew that earth was past the point where it could survive itself. The ships seemed to be humanity's only hope.

So the ships had scattered outward from the solar system. Only three years into their centuries-long voyages, they heard earth's last radio transmissions telling of the nuclear destruction of New York and Beijing and Tokyo and Baghdad and Jerusalem and Moscow and Johannesburg and Rio de Janeiro. They listened to claims of victory in different languages — and then there was silence. The ships moved on through the interstellar night. Eventually they were so far separated from one another that they lost contact. Each ship moved on alone.

Our story takes place on a small green-blue planet, partly covered with clouds, which circles near the warmth of a medium-sized yellow star. There is a little human colony here, trying to establish a foothold for what may be the last members of the human race. The planet is somewhat like the earth which their ancestors left 1,000 years ago, an earth that they know about only from their computer library. This world has sparse vegetation and some fish in the seas, but very little animal life has been found on the land. The few humans are finding life hard. The ship was stocked with all the latest technology, but the voyage of centuries pushed its resources to their limit, and survival is a struggle.

They have few causes for celebration and no time for vacations or holidays. All the old religious and political holidays were left behind anyway. But, sometimes in the evening, they gather around the telescope and take turns looking at the star around which the radioactive earth circles:

> *If I forget you, O Jerusalem, let my right hand wither!*
> *Let my tongue cling to the roof of my mouth, if I do not*
> *remember you, if I do not set Jerusalem above my highest joy!*

On one cool morning, two of the colonists are making their way through the mountains that stretch away from the little settlement. They don't have enough skilled people or working equipment to make a really good survey of the planet, so the exploration of the planet has to be done largely the old-fashioned way, on foot. The planet has very little good farmland and few mineral resources, and it's important to pinpoint just where those things might be. And there is always a thought in the back of some of the colonists' minds — "Maybe we aren't really alone here."

So, John and Mary are making their way through the hills, taking soil samples and studying outcroppings of rock, and as they go, they talk.

"Maybe so," Mary said. "There might be more minerals here than we think, and perhaps we'll be able to find fuel and other resources that we need. But that still isn't any sign that things are going to work out for people here in the long run. We came here by accident and we could all get killed by accident. It would be comforting to think there's some overall force for good in the universe, but that doesn't mean there is one."

"Well," John said, "I can't believe that all of life is completely pointless. If the ships hadn't left earth when they did, the whole human race would have been wiped out. But we made it. We're here! Are you going to tell me that was just a coincidence?"

"Of course!" she said. "And if that coincidence hadn't happened, we wouldn't be here to talk about it. There's nothing mysterious about that. It was unlikely, and lucky for us, but that doesn't prove there's any higher power. There's no purpose to the universe, nothing arranging matters so that humanity survives and prospers. Or if there is, it isn't doing a very good job!"

"There's no way I can make you see it my way. I can't *prove* that there's some purpose to life. I just have a deep gut feeling that life is more than an accident or a bad joke. Our mothers and fathers wouldn't have had the courage to start the voyage if they hadn't felt that way."

"I suppose that's right," Mary said. "Our ancestors and people in a few other ships — and those others are probably all dead now. Is that the purpose of life — billions get killed so a few thousand can fly off into exile, and most of them are now dust floating between the stars? Sorry — I just can't buy it."

During the conversation they were working their way up a ridge, through the thin grass and a few scraggly bushes. The ground was rocky and they had to watch their footing carefully. Sometimes they would stop to take soil samples and make notes, or swing the video camera around the landscape. They were getting tired as they approached the top of the ridge.

"If that's the way you feel," John asked, "why go on? Why keep on living, why push yourself out here, if you think that all of life is a pointless accident?"

"I don't know," she said. "I guess I just have to be as honest as I can. The universe is empty except for us, and soon we may be gone, too. But I like living better than being dead, so I keep going for as long as I can."

"Do you think there's no other intelligent life in the universe? That earth is the only planet where it evolved?"

"That's what it looks like."

"But there's life here — and with life, intelligence would have to develop sooner or later."

"That doesn't follow. The fish here might never come out of the water — and probably won't now that we've arrived. Even if life develops on a planet, maybe nothing will happen to make bigger brains an advantage for survival."

John started to reply as they neared the top of the ridge, but suddenly Mary silenced him in mid-sentence and pointed. Up in front of them rose a thin curl of smoke.

Very quietly, they came over the top and stopped, hiding behind a boulder and scanning the other side of the ridge with automatically stabilized binoculars. The smoke came from the shore of a little lake at the bottom of the ridge, about a mile away. Through the binoculars they could see a small fire burning. There was some wood there — and there was a figure, humanoid, sitting on a rock next to the fire. As they watched, it reached out a stick and seemed to turn a couple of brown objects near the flames.

John slipped back down out of sight and pulled out the radio to check with the colony. A moment's conversation showed that all the colonists were accounted for. Nobody else should have been in the area. "Well," John said, "we've spotted something. An animal — looks humanoid from this distance. It may be — intelligent." The radio crackled with questions and sarcasm.

"Like it or not, it's there. No — don't send the chopper out. It'd scare the thing off. I'll keep this channel open while we go down to check. Of *course* we'll be careful!"

"So much for being alone," he said to Mary as they got out their weapons and checked them. They'd never needed to use the old nine-millimeter automatics, but were glad they had them now.

"Okay — maybe there are two intelligent races lost in the universe," she said nervously. They started down the slope as quietly as they could, separating to approach the figure from opposite sides. It still sat there quietly as they approached, looking at the fire.

Mary's brain raced as she came in quietly from one side. Too many things to think about — what kind of gesture of peace to make, how to fire quickly if the thing attacked, and how to try to communicate if it *was* intelligent and didn't run away or kill them. The same kinds of thoughts raced through John's head as he approached from the other side. He knew that his heartbeat and his rapid, almost panicky, breathing could be heard over the radio link back at the colony. Sure he was afraid! What ever made him think he wanted to meet any other life form? It would be better to be alone and safe.

When they were about thirty meters away, the figure looked up and spotted Mary. It stood up and swung its head around and saw John, who had stopped dead. As it stood, they could see that it was indeed humanoid. In fact, it seemed to be a rather dark-complexioned young man. John and Mary both clicked off the safeties on their weapons.

Then, "Do you have any food?" it called. He was speaking their language! "Do you have anything to eat?" he called again. "If you do, bring it. We can share."

The radio was crackling at John's side but he didn't notice it. He and Mary both walked toward the young man by the fire, almost in a daze. He had removed what they could now see were a couple of round loaves from a rock beside the fire. Their weapons slipped back into their holsters almost automatically.

"Come and have breakfast," the young man said, and stretched out both hands to them with bread in each. His sleeves slipped back as he reached out to them, and they could see that his wrists bore fresh scars of what seemed to be some deep wound.

For thus says the Lord GOD: "I myself will search for my sheep, and will seek them out. As shepherds seek out their flocks when they are among their scattered sheep, so I will seek out my sheep. I will rescue them

from all the places to which they have been scattered
on a day of clouds and thick darkness."

— Ezekiel 34:11-12

Comment

The text from Ezekiel is the Old Testament reading for Christ The King Sunday, the last Sunday of the church year for Year A in the Revised Common Lectionary. It is part of God's promise to the exiles in Babylon after the destruction of Jerusalem — a situation that also evoked Psalm 137, which is quoted earlier in this story. Exiles from some future destruction of the earth would seem to be in an even more hopeless situation than were those Jews carried off a few hundred miles from their homeland.

It may seem fairly obvious that the appearance of Christ to John and Mary at the end of the story is based on John 21:9-14. This is, in fact, the case, but as the climax of this story the biblical account has been mediated through the conclusion of C. S. Lewis' *The Voyage of the "Dawn Treader"* (New York: Collier, 1970), pp. 214-215. There the image from the Gospel of John is used in a somewhat different but related way.

Chapter Six

Hope In Heaven

Ezekiel 34:1 1-16, 20-24

Eighty years out from earth, the ship crept between the stars. Though it would achieve a tenth of light speed, another century and a half would pass before its journey ended. Three miles long, the ship was a little world to itself.

Juanita Lopez walked slowly along the corridor. Usually friendly, today she hardly noticed the people she met. Her inner eye was fixed on the baby in the ship's clinic, the baby who should not have been born. Now the decision was hers as the ship's chief medical officer: Genetic contamination or purity? Life or death?

She came almost automatically to her destination, the small building in the park where she could think quietly. There was seldom anyone there. Some called it "the chapel," though it had no official name. Many people back on earth had opposed sending any sign at all of religion on the first voyage to the stars, and no preference could be shown to any of earth's faiths. So the chapel was simply a plain room with a few chairs and symbols on its walls — the star of David, the calm Buddha, and others. It was the calmness that helped when she had problems to solve or decisions to make. The Yin-Yang flow or the purity of the Zoroastrian flame spoke in mysterious ways of a hope for peace.

Juanita sank into a chair and thought back to the clinic. She couldn't forget the look of that baby — not quite normal, but so close that nothing had been noticed at first. They simply had assumed that all the prenatal tests would catch any problems, and of course all of the shippers had to have a clean genetic record. All the old hereditary diseases were supposed to be history. Her assistant, Jack Williams, had done some careful detective work to track down the difficulty.

"A small error in the DNA," he said, looking at the computer screen. "Might be from the increased cosmic radiation, though we

39

can't be sure. There were no obvious physical signs. The chemical tests from amniocentesis should have picked it up, but somehow we missed it. Maybe we've gotten overconfident."

"It may be a small error," she said, "But the child's development shows severe brain deficiencies — what they called mental retardation back on earth, and there could be physical problems as well."

"Yes," said Jack. "It shouldn't have been born. And now, at six months...."

His voice had trailed off, but Juanita knew what he meant. Could they put a child that age to death? But could it be allowed to live? What kind of sign would that be for the shippers? For generations they had learned that people have a right to genetic health and a duty to maintain it. This wasn't a decision she wanted to make. Doctors were supposed to save life. And they were supposed to ensure that all lives were healthy.

Life had been so different on earth. How much simpler their decisions must have been! She opened her eyes and looked around the chapel. Like most of the shippers, she had gotten only the vaguest ideas about the old religions — a few comments in school, or odds and ends in conversations. But she thought now how comforting it must have been to think that there was some benevolent God up in heaven taking care of things. How easy to have such a God who would always tell you what decisions to make! Now, however, the ship was traveling through the heavens, and all that was left of those old beliefs were these ancient symbols. At least they were able to give her an irrational sense of peace and security.

All but the one she didn't like to look at.

It was a man nailed to a piece of wood, his bleeding body twisted in pain. It was bad enough to have to see those few in the clinic who were sick or hurt. But this! Someone had told her that this was supposed to be *God*. God abandoned, suffering, and dying. There was no peace and security there.

God thrown away by society? God killed? This man nailed to the wood?

If there were a God (just suppose) then would any life be without hope? Would even death be hopeless? (You're in interstellar space, Juanita! We recycle the bodies of our dead, so that none of the valuable chemicals will be wasted. This is no place for myths.) Was this lonely, dying man supposed to be a sign of *hope*? For whom?

For me, destined to die and have my body reduced to atoms light years from home?

For a damaged baby whose life seems pointless in this little bubble of health creeping between the stars? What seems pointless to me would be no barrier to that God on the wood (if there is any God).

Why should a scientist, of all people, think that answers could always be easy?

She rose to go, to act. Peace seemed a long way off, but it might be real peace.

> *For thus says the Lord GOD: "I myself will search for my sheep, and will seek them out. As shepherds seek out their flocks when they are among their scattered sheep, so I will seek out my sheep. I will rescue them from all the places to which they have been scattered on a day of clouds and thick darkness."*
>
> — Ezekiel 34:11-12

Comment

This story sermon was originally published in George L. Murphy, LaVonne Althouse, and Russell Willis' book, *Cosmic Witness* (Lima, Ohio: CSS Publishing Company, 1996), pp. 177-179, and is used here, with minor changes, by permission. It is connected with the same text from Ezekiel that inspired the previous sermon, "The Exiles." Here the "exile" is self-imposed, but the sense of cosmic loneliness in this setting would be no less real.

This story could also be used with Jesus' parable of the lost sheep (Matthew 18:12-14 and Luke 15:4-7). But, that parable itself should be seen as having as part of its background the picture of God seeking out the sheep to "rescue them from all the places to which they have been scattered on a day of clouds and thick darkness" — as well as a number of other shepherd passages in the Old Testament.

Chapter Seven

"I'll Be Back!"

Matthew 24:36-44

Nightfall at Lod airport, 25 miles northeast of Jerusalem. Night, and the 200-plus passengers aboard the new jumbo jet sitting all alone out in the middle of one runway may have seen the last daylight of their lives. Terrorists are in control throughout the plane and others are on guard around it — no one knows how many. The Israeli security forces have been studying the situation all day and have decided that they have no chance of taking the plane by force without losing almost everyone on board.

The outside world has almost ceased to exist for the passengers and crew. They are allowed no communication with the tower. The passengers don't know what is going on up in the first-class cabin which the hijackers have cleared, and where many of them are gathered now with the officers and flight attendants. In the confusion and panic, no one has noticed that one of the passengers, a young man who looks as if he's probably a rabbinical student, is missing. He is up front with the terrorists, where he seems to be the center of attention.

Nobody is very clear about these hijackers — about who they are, what they represent, or what their demands are. But one thing is clear: They're planning to blow up the plane and kill everyone aboard if they don't get what they want by dawn. The ransom has to be paid by sunrise.

But what is the ransom? Only this young man who walks with a slight limp seems to know. He sits calmly in one of the seats as the hijackers surround him, shouting demands and threats about what will happen if he can't deliver. Whatever the ransom is — money, or release of prisoners, or military information — he seems an unlikely person to produce it. But he is the only one who seems to have any hope that he can come through with the ransom before dawn.

The officers and flight attendants are told that the passengers will have to be ready to leave the plane immediately if the ransom is actually delivered. There can be absolutely no waiting. No explanation is given for this, but they know that they have to be ready. These terrorists don't look like the kind of people to make empty threats.

Finally the young man stands up and turns to the hostages who are standing uncertainly at the front of the cabin. "I don't know exactly when, but I'll be back. Keep the people calm, but keep them alert. Tell them I'll be back — and tell them to stay awake!"

Then he motions to the terrorists, and even though they're the ones holding the guns and grenades, he seems to be the one in control of the situation. A few of the passengers catch a glimpse of him as he starts down the steps. Then he's gone, and the main cabin door is slammed shut. Flight attendants start to move down the aisles, explaining to passengers a few at a time that they have to be calm, that help is on the way, and that they must stay alert and be ready to leave at a moment's notice. They repeat the young man's words over and over and say, "You can trust him. Stay awake. Watch."

There are different reactions to these words. One elderly man keeps repeating to those around him, "I'm glad there's at least one person we can trust." But a few rows back a woman argues with a friend. "There's no reason to believe anyone is going to pay their ransom. Who is this guy who's supposed to save our lives? Have you seen him? This so-called ransomer is just a story these stewardesses have made up to keep us quiet. That's their job."

From the time that the outside door closed, only half an hour passes before a man looks at his watch for the tenth time, shouts, "He's never coming back!" and bolts for the door. He actually makes it almost halfway down the ladder before there's a burst of machine gun fire and then a heavy silence.

Excited talk breaks out all over the plane. "He was crazy to try that," says a man near the back. "We have to trust that that fellow is coming back to save us. He said he would."

"Doesn't look like he's helped us much so far," says his neighbor. "How long can you go on blindly trusting someone you haven't even seen? How do you know you can trust him at all?"

"You can't survive if you don't believe in anything," answers the first man angrily. "I have a friend I would literally trust with my life. If he says he'll do something, no matter how hard, I know it's as good as done. That's what I mean by trust."

"Yeah, but you don't know this guy who's supposed to be bringing the ransom. You never met him — never saw him. All you know is what these flight attendants tell you. Is that something we can bet our lives on?"

Before the first man can answer, a woman in the row ahead of them twists around in her seat. "I'll tell you this about 'trust,' " she says bitterly. "When I got married, my husband promised, 'to be faithful to you, until death parts us.' Last month I found out he was having an affair with my best friend, and now he wants a divorce. That's how much you can trust people! I'm never going to make a fool of myself again by trusting anyone."

"That's right, and every minute we sit here trusting, there's less reason to think we'll be saved. We're just a minute closer to the end."

"No," says the man who had spoken first. "I think that every minute we wait we're closer to being saved."

It's past midnight now, and outside there are sudden shouts and challenges, an answer, and a knock on the door. Everyone watches as the door opens. They see a young man — who is one of the terrorists. There are groans and angry cries of "I told you so" from the cynics who had secretly begun to hope that it might really be true.

The believers are quiet now, not having the heart to argue. The flight attendants start going around the cabin again, repeating the young man's message: "I don't know exactly when, but I'll be back. Stay awake." A few people nod and smile and whisper to their neighbors.

The minutes drag on. One man keeps dozing off and his wife has to shake him. "He said to stay awake," she whispers angrily. "Can't you stay awake for just a few hours?"

"Ah, it's all nonsense anyway," he mutters. "They're just trying to scare us. Why don't they at least break out the liquor so we can enjoy ourselves?"

Up in the first-class cabin a hijacker laughs at one of the flight attendants who has sat down wearily for a moment's rest. "You're a fool to think that he'll really take the risk of coming back to save you. Why are you wasting your time trying to get all these people to believe in him? Nobody risks his life to help someone else. You're all as good as dead."

"Do you want it to come to that?" she asks slowly. "Do you want to have to kill all of us — including the children in there? You'd be on the run for the rest of your life. Maybe you're hoping he will come back so you don't have to do it. I think maybe he's coming to save you as well as us — to save you from yourself."

"You're crazy! I don't need anyone to save me. Here's my savior," he shouts, waving his gun in her face. They glare at each other for a moment, and then he turns and walks away.

Nearly three o'clock in the morning now — people are drowsy and restless. Suddenly, there are noises outside — cars, people running, and shouts. Passengers look out the window and some begin to cry, "It's him!" They start standing up and looking toward the exits, but then there are bursts of gunfire and screams. "They've killed him!" a woman yells, falling hopelessly back into her seat. "No," says her husband, "it could have been someone else."

"It could have been," he repeats in a low voice.

The door opens and a terrorist from outside looks in. "Was it him?" "What happened?" "Is he coming?" they all clamor — but there is no answer. He only looks at them coldly and slams the door again. The hijackers move about the plane, ordering people back into their seats.

Everybody is subdued as the minutes tick by. "Well," says the woman who had refused to believe in the young man's existence, "do you still believe after all this? I told you that stuff about someone coming to save us was just a story to keep us quiet. You see?"

"Yes, I still believe he'll come," says a man across the aisle.

"You do, do you? No doubts at all? Come on — what's the point of pretending anymore?"

46

"Yes, I believe," he says. "But — no, I'm not sure. He said he'd come back. But...."

"Doesn't sound like a very strong faith," she sneers. He has no answer.

There are some sporadic gunshots outside — maybe just terrorists who are nervous. Faint traces of light begin to appear in the sky and the flight attendants make efforts to reassure those who are on the edge of panic. They try to wake others who are dozing off, reminding them of the promise: "I'll be back. Stay awake."

The sky is getting pink in the east. The hijackers are talking on their radios now, checking their ammo clips and moving to block off the exits. People have their faces against the windows, peering out desperately. The hijacker who had argued with the flight attendant is standing at the main cabin door. There is no expression on his face as he looks over the cabin. Then he pauses, as if listening.

There is another knock at the door.

Comment

This is not terribly "science-fiction," but has more the character of a suspense story or perhaps an "action movie." Those categories aren't, however, mutually exclusive. The technological elements in the story may be enough to qualify it for this collection. The story could be placed in a futuristic setting at a spaceport on the moon but nothing would really be gained by that, and the familiarity of hijacking and hostage situations on earth, especially those involving Israel, would be lost.

This sermon was originally given before the events of September 11, 2001, and the most recent rounds of fighting in the Middle East. The terrorist attack on America gave public perceptions of hijacking an even more ominous character than they had before and has introduced an explicitly religious element. Some updating to bring in reference to the terrorist attacks on America might be attempted but this shouldn't obscure the eschatological thrust of the text.

The theological concern addressed here is that of "the delay of the parousia," the fact that the return of Christ did not happen

47

within a few years after Easter, as some of the texts of the New Testament seem to expect. If we consider the matter on a cosmological time scale, however, and realize that 2,000 years is a very small period in comparison with something like fourteen billion years that have elapsed since the big bang, this delay is put in perspective. The text from Matthew (which is the Gospel Reading for the First Sunday In Advent in Year A in the Revised Common Lectionary) emphasizes that the time of the end is known only to the Father. It encourages not speculation about when this will be but watchfulness, "for the Son of Man is coming at an unexpected hour" (v. 44).

Chapter Eight

Time Travel

Mark 1:12-15

The Spirit hurled Jesus into the desert. Fresh from the joy and exaltation of his baptism, fresh from hearing the heavenly voice which said, "You are my Son, the Beloved" — just when he was coming up out of the water, the Spirit seized Jesus and drove him into the wilderness. He could hardly move fast enough to keep up — running, walking to catch his breath. Out — away from people, away from villages, into the rocky open spaces. He went back to where his fathers and mothers had lived centuries before. Back to the wandering in the wilderness, back — for forty days, always farther back, and farther away.

It was, as the book says, "A howling wilderness waste." There was nothing there but rock and sand. Nothing but the hot winds of the day and the cold winds of the night, and the sounds and cries of the desert beasts — the birds, the crawling things. The birds circling high overhead and the snakes slithering across the rock — always back.

He awoke in the long ago. He was clothed in skins and furs that scratched and smelled bad, but didn't keep the icy wind out very well. He sat beside a small fire where a few chunks of the woolly mammoth's flesh were roasting. His few companions were exhausted after the violent hunt that had ended with two of them dead. They had had enough to eat for the first time in weeks, and were full and sleepy. The rest of them were snoring loudly. A cold wind blew down from the ice fields a few miles to the north, bearing more snow.

Then he heard a snuffling sound, and looked out into the darkness. Soon a single scrawny wolf appeared at the edge of the firelight. It must have been starving to come close to humans; it must have smelled the food. Maybe it had followed the trail of blood from the hunt.

Without thinking, he had reached for his spear. The message in his brain had been automatic: Beast — enemy — kill. Humans had to kill wolves, just as wolves always had to kill humans. He gripped the spear, but then he stopped and looked at the starving wolf. The beast did not look at him. It was gazing at the pieces of uncooked meat that lay on the rock beside him. And he thought, "It's hungry, too — just the way we were yesterday."

Very slowly, he speared a piece of the meat, and very slowly he reached it out to the beast. The wolf just watched, but its tongue hung out. The man lowered the dripping meat from the end of his spear to the ground. The wolf approached, slowly, warily — then suddenly seized the chunk and raced out of the firelight. The next night, however, he was back, at the edge of the darkness. And this time he approached the man a little more quickly, and came a bit nearer.

But that would be too late. He had to go farther back.

He crouched behind a tree — one of a small group of trees on the vast rolling plains of Africa. A few other humans crouched beside him, hidden as if in wait for game. They clutched stones that had been chipped to make rough hand axes. Beasts were coming.

These were the beasts that they hated, not just the ones they hunted for food. These were beasts that looked like humans, and who walked erect like humans — but they were just beasts. They were different from humans.

The beasts who walked erect looked like humans at a distance, but up close their skins were seen to be pale, and their foreheads were more sloped. They had no hand axes — only sharp sticks. The grunts they made to each other were different from the grunts of the humans. They were different. They were beasts who had fought with the humans before. They had to be killed.

Now the beast people were coming quietly through the grass, each one looking carefully for edible roots or perhaps some bird eggs or a lizard for food. They were so intent on their search that they did not pick up the scent of the humans, crouched behind the trees. Quickly, at his command, the humans surrounded the beasts-who-looked-human, the fists bearing their axes raised. Sharpened sticks were raised in defiance.

Then, before he could give the command to strike, he happened to look into the eyes of one of the beast people. He saw there the same hate, the same fear, that he had seen in the eyes of his people — in the eyes of humans. The eyes into which he looked were strange in color and shape, but they were human eyes. Slowly, he lowered his fist. His people looked questioningly at him and grunted, "Kill? Kill?" But no one moved. Then the stranger in front of him slowly lowered his spear and looked at him. Carefully, deliberately, he dropped his axe to the ground. He held out his hands, palms up. The stranger held his spear level for a moment and tensed his muscles — then dropped it and held out his hands.

But that would be too late. He had to go farther back.

Nearly 100 million years ago, no humans walked the earth. The dinosaurs ruled the world. The huge 100-foot-long brontosaurus placidly chewed the tops of the trees; the terrible carnivore tyrannosaurus rex, "tyrant lizard king," ran down its prey on its two hind legs like some caricature of a human, tearing apart whatever it caught with teeth like butcher knives.

Humans had not yet evolved. But this human walked along a path in the garden in the shade of the trees, looking for some fruit for a midday meal. He passed one tree in the center of the garden and saw that its fruit was ripe and beautiful — but of course *that* tree was out of bounds. He started to walk on.

Suddenly a huge form reared up and stepped out into the open beside that special tree. It was tyrannosaurus rex. The tyrant lizard looked down at the little human, and bent its huge head down, and opened its jaws with those butcher-knife teeth — and spoke.

"This is a beautiful tree, isn't it?" asked the dinosaur.

"Yes, it is," said the human.

"Mmm — beautiful fruit, too. Looks as if it's just ripe for picking. If I weren't carnivorous, I'd probably eat some." Then tyrannosaurus paused. "Tell me," it went on, "is it really true that God told you not to eat from *any* tree of the garden?"

"No," said the human. "Just from this one. 'In the day that you eat of it you shall die.' "

"Uh-huh," said the tyrant. "I see. That's interesting. You know — I'll bet you wouldn't really *die* if you ate some of this fruit! That's probably kind of an exaggeration, don't you think?" The human said nothing.

"In fact, probably nothing would happen if you ate some of this fruit. God just wants to be able to give you an order — *any* order — and have you obey it. Kind of to keep you in your place, you know. And so if you did eat — you'd be just as good as God. It would be like saying you could tell right from wrong yourself, without any arbitrary rules. God wants to keep you toeing the line, but you can make your own decisions."

The man looked at the tree and looked at the beautiful fruit and said, "No." And he started to walk on.

"Wait a minute, wait a minute," yelled tyrannosaurus as he loped after the human. It jumped onto the path in front of him.

"Look," said the dinosaur, its voice no longer so friendly. "Perhaps I didn't make myself clear. Maybe you don't understand who I am. I'm the king. I rule this world. Nobody defies me. God can give all the orders he likes, but I'm the one who has the power here. If you know what's good for you, you'll go back and eat some of that fruit!" Then the dinosaur voice, with an effort, became friendly again: "Be reasonable. You're hungry and...."

"No," said the man, and walked on.

"You'll never get away with this," the tyrant screamed after him. "Nobody disobeys the king! I'm not finished with you yet!"

Jesus turned around and smiled grimly, smiled for the first time in forty days. And then he walked forward.

"And the angels waited on him."

Comment

One of the important influences on the development of this story was Charles L. Harness' book, *The Paradox Men*. (A short version of this was published in 1949 and it appeared as half of one of the old Ace "double novels" in 1955. An updated version with accompanying essays by George Zebrowski and Brian Aldiss and an "Author's Note" was published by Crown in 1984 as Volume 7 in the "Classics of Modern Science Fiction" series.) Here, as global nuclear war begins in the twenty-second century, the death of the mysterious hero Alar plunges him back in time to the beginnings of the human race to change the very nature of human consciousness and the direction of evolution.

But the idea of "recapitulation" is a significant biblical theme, and that is the immediate point of contact with the biblical stories of the temptation of Christ. In Matthew and Luke's versions, Jesus can be seen as "doing over again right" the testing of Israel in the wilderness. In the shorter Marcan story, he seems to go back to the situation of Adam "with the wild beasts" in Eden.

This story sermon was originally published in George L. Murphy, LaVonne Althouse, and Russell Willis' book, *Cosmic Witness* (Lima, Ohio: CSS Publishing Company, 1996), pp.179-183, and is used here, with minor revisions, by permission. I am not an expert on dinosaurs, and a colleague later pointed out to me that the brontosaurus and tyrannosaurus were not contemporaries. But I decided to leave this as it was originally published. (I was actually more interested in the resonance of the "tyrant lizard king" with the serpent of Genesis 3, who is identified in Revelation 12:9 with the dragon who persecutes the people of God and the Messiah.)

Biblical verses that are quoted from in the sermon are, respectively, Mark 1:11; Deuteronomy 32:10; Genesis 2:17; and Mark 1:13.

Chapter Nine

The Aliens Are Puzzled

John 10:11-16

The aliens didn't come to conquer the earth. They came just to survive. It was an old species that long ago had discovered interstellar travel and were able to range throughout the galaxy to find all the physical resources they needed. They didn't lack for anything in that way.

But they were also a very tired species. They had been through everything, experienced all that the universe had to offer, and there was really nothing left to do. They had extended their lives to the limit that was scientifically possible — and anyway, what was the point of a longer life if nothing new could be done? They knew that the universe would continue to spread out and cool down, and they couldn't see anything hopeful about that.

So they had come to one of the few planets in the galaxy that had borne an intelligent species, a species that had developed very quickly. The aliens wanted to know — is there any way we can recapture some sense of youth, some excitement in life?

Their cloaked ship had orbited the earth, invisible to sensors from the planet, while the scout ships went down to explore some sites that had been selected. Now the away-teams had returned and were reporting to the commander and her staff.

Team A (of course they didn't use our alphabet — I'm translating as best I can) was the first to report. They had observed the political process in one of the areas of the planet.

"They are now trying to choose a leader for the humans in that country," reported the team leader. "We assumed that they would have some objective procedure for determining the abilities of people, and select one who was well qualified and with some clearly specified plans. Apparently that is not the case. The person who is chosen will be the one who tells people repeatedly that he is good and that the other candidates are bad."

"Do any of the candidates have any vision for the future of their country?" asked the commander.

"Many of them speak about that while they are trying to be chosen," said the team leader, "but usually nothing comes of it once they are elected. They spend a great deal of time raising money and arguing about flags."

"That is not very encouraging," said the science officer. "What about Team B?" That had seemed to be their best bet, the observers who had gone to a big scientific establishment. The team leader stood up to report. "It is a laboratory for research and development in genetics. They expect to make a breakthrough that will enable them to extend the life of each of these humans to 200 of their years."

"Our species long ago exceeded that life span," said the science officer.

"Of course," said the commander. "But they are just beginning. More to the point — do they have any idea what they will do with longer lives?"

"We could not see that they were giving much thought to that question," answered the team leader. "They seemed to be interested only in solving the scientific problem."

"Many of them do seem to have a great deal of leisure time," said the leader of Team C. "At the site to which we were assigned, there were thousands of humans at something called a baseball game. It was some sort of contest with very complicated rules that we were not able to understand."

"Thousands all engaged in this contest?" asked the commander.

"No — there were only a few actually playing. The rest were watching and making noise, apparently encouraging what they called 'their team.' We were puzzled by that because the teams were actually owned by some wealthy person and the services of the players were traded from one team to another. We could not understand why those who were watching felt a deep sense of commitment to these paid performers."

"Quite illogical," said the science officer. "I am not optimistic that we can learn anything from this strange species."

"I agree," said the security officer. "And I have no hope at all that we'll get anything of value from our final away-team. We decided long ago that religion is a waste of time. Our species once had ideas about an all-powerful being who demanded obedience and worship and promised rewards and life after death, but we outgrew that. We learned that we had to ensure our own survival."

"Initially we thought that as well," reported the leader of the final away-team. "The religious group in the worship service that we observed did speak of an all-powerful God. But they also spoke about this God *dying*."

"How could that be?" asked the commander. "How could an all-powerful being die? And why would a God allow that to happen?"

"Apparently, this God is supposed to have become human and to have died in order to save his people. It was not very clear to us, but it seems that in their sacred text, God spoke of 'laying down his life' for his sheep — which apparently is a metaphor for humans. And this God is supposed to be alive now even though he was killed."

"But that makes no sense! It's just the opposite of what a religion is supposed to be!" exclaimed the security officer. "Creatures are supposed to serve their God and be willing to die for him — not the other way around."

"Of course," said the science officer. "It does go against common sense. But we have learned that common sense is not always a reliable guide. Suppose for the sake of argument that there were a God who was willing to die to save creatures. There might be some purpose to life in such a world. Death would not have the last word — if that is possible."

"We weren't sent here just to study the customs of another species," said the commander. "We were to see if this species had anything that might give hope to our civilization. Could this strange idea about a God who became human and 'laid down his life' mean anything for us?"

"Our scholars will have to study the data more fully," replied the team leader. "But the sacred text that they read ended with some words that made us ask the same question."

*I have other sheep that do not belong to this fold. I
must bring them also, and they will listen to my voice.
So there will be one flock, one shepherd.*

— John 10:16

Comment

Christian claims that the Son of God was uniquely incarnated in Jesus of Nazareth have sometimes been criticized because they seem to give unwarranted importance to one species on one small planet in a vast universe. What about all the other intelligent species that might exist on other planets and that might be in need of salvation? The uses of the word "might" in that challenge should be noted: At present we don't know that there is life, let alone intelligence, beyond the earth, and if it does exist we know nothing about the state of its relationship with God. Nevertheless, some consideration should be given to the question. It would be very short-sighted for the church to put off any consideration of it until the first unambiguous signal from other intelligent beings arrives at the earth.

This isn't the first time such questions have been asked. How is a Jewish Messiah relevant to Gentiles? How can a church that evolved in a European setting welcome people from the rest of the world? Does a message of salvation for human beings offer any hope for other terrestrial species? The ways in which some of these questions have been dealt with may help us to think about the relevance of the gospel for extraterrestrials — if there are any.

It is extremely unlikely that the language of John 10:16, whether it is understood as coming from the lips of Jesus or as a composition of the evangelist, had extraterrestrials in mind. It is much more probable that it refers to Gentile believers or perhaps to Christians in a later setting who were separated for one reason or another from the Johannine community. (cf. Raymond E. Brown, *The Community of the Beloved Disciple* [New York: Paulist Press, 1979], p. 90.) In fact, in the story I don't claim that this verse does have extraterrestrials in mind, but if extraterrestrials were struck by other aspects of the fourth gospel, this verse would be likely at least to raise the question of whether or not the Christ proclaimed by that gospel might mean something for them, too.

Chapter Ten

Burying The Seeds

John 12:20-33

She sat on the ground and watched the grass grow. The long green stalks were not good to eat. The grains at the top were food. They could be eaten when they turned brown. It took a long time for the grains to grow. She knew this because she had been with the other women for many days. They gathered grain and fruit and roots that could be eaten. It was hard work. There was never enough. There were only a few places where the right kinds of grass grew. Sometimes animals or birds came and ate the grain before it was ripe.

The men were farther away from camp. They were hunting. That was hard work, too. They snuck up on an animal to kill it with a spear or a stone. Often they brought back nothing. Then all the tribe had to eat was a little grain that had been saved. Soon, they might have to move on. They had to find a place with animals and grass with grains they could eat. They would do that if they could live through the winter.

In winter they were afraid. People died then. There was never enough to eat. They wrapped themselves in animal skins and sat around fires. But they were cold and hungry in winter. Their only food then was grain they had saved. It would keep through the winter, even when the grass had died and turned brown.

She had wondered where the grass went in the winter. What happened to the flowers and the other plants? The earth had died. Then after many cold days grass would grow in the fields again. Leaves would come on the trees and the animals returned. None of the other people seemed to think about those things. Where did the grass go in the winter when it died? How did it come back?

It was not only the grass that died in the winter. People died. Her son had died. She could not do anything. His head became hot and he coughed and cried, and became still. It had been hard to bury him in the cold ground. She had seen many of the people die, but the death of the boy scared her. It made her sad. That was when she began to wonder about the grass, and the way the earth died.

Now it was early in the morning. The other women were working. They were gathering food where they could find it. She stayed near the camp, watching her special plants. The other women knew not to touch them after she spoke loudly to them about it. They left her plants alone. But they thought that she was foolish. What foolish things she talked about! But she did not care what they thought. She had seen something that they had not seen.

It had been more than a year ago. She was coming back to camp after a day of gathering. She had found a lot of grain. Her stone jar was almost full. When she was almost to the camp, she tripped over a root. She fell, and the grain spilled out of her jar. She tried to gather it up, but much was lost. It was buried in the dirt. She was angry, but she could not do anything. She brought what she had and forgot about her fall. But in the spring she remembered.

One day, the winter was past and the grass began to grow again. She walked past the place where she had spilled the grain. Near the root that had tripped her there were many blades of young grass. Women never knew where the grass would grow. But this was where she had spilled the grain. She thought about that for a long time. Maybe the grass grew because she spilled the grain.

She did not tell anyone else. She watched the new grass grow during the summer. She went with the other women to gather grain and fruit. But she always watched this special place. She scared the birds away. When the grains were brown, she gathered them all. She gathered much more than she had spilled. She did not take it all to eat, or save for winter. She carried some of the grain to another place and dropped it on the ground. She covered it with dirt. She did not really know why she did that.

During the winter she was often sorry that she had put grain in the ground. She could have eaten it during the cold days when she was hungry. The men could find no animals and the little children were crying for food. She thought of the brown bits of grain lying in the dirt, cold and hard. She had been foolish. The grain was dead now. It was like her son.

But they lived through the winter. Spring came. It was warm again, and the plants began to grow. She went to see where she had buried the grain. There were many more little green blades coming out of the ground.

Now the grain was ripe, and winter was coming again. One evening, as they sat around the fire, there was talk of moving the camp. "We cannot find animals," the men said. "We must find a place where grain is growing," the other women said. Then she spoke.

"I know where the grain goes in the winter," she said.

"Do not be foolish," said the other women. "We must find the grain. No one knows where it will grow."

"I know," she said. "The pieces of grain fall into the ground and die in the winter. But in the spring they are alive and grow. They make more grain."

The men laughed. The women said, "That is foolish. Why would you think something like that?"

"Because I have seen it," she said. It was hard to find the words for the new things which she thought. She told them about spilling the grain, and about the new grain she found in the spring. "I buried some grain in the ground and it grew," she said. "We will eat it this winter. And I buried more. It will grow next year."

"You buried food in the ground?" they said. "You threw it away. You are a very foolish woman. Where is the grain? We will go and dig it up. We will need food in the winter."

"No," she said. "We will always need food. But if grain dies, it will give us more grain." They yelled at her and made threats. But she would not tell them where the grain was buried.

That winter was very hard for her. The people were angry with her. When they had little food they would not give her a share. "Go dig up your grain," they laughed. They called her "Woman who buries food in the dirt." It was a long winter. She was very lonely.

The spring came. They could find food. The rest of the people forgot about the grain buried in the ground. But she did not forget.

One summer morning they sat around the fire at dawn. She said, "Do you remember the grain that I buried in the ground?" Some did not remember. But she led them out of the camp to a place on a hillside. Many stalks of grass, heavy with grain, stood in the sunshine.

The other women were very surprised. They had never seen so much grain all growing in the same place. "How did you find this?" they asked her.

"I knew it would be here," she said. "Unless the grain falls into the ground and dies, it is just a little grain. But if it dies, it makes much grain."

The other people were very happy. "Now we will not be so hungry in the winter," they said. They were laughing and smiling. But the woman who had buried the grain had become very thoughtful again. She was thinking about her son.

> *Very truly, I tell you, unless a grain of wheat falls into the earth and dies, it remains just a single grain; but if it dies, it bears much fruit. Those who love their life lose it, and those who hate their life in this world will keep it for eternal life.* — John 12:24-25

Comment

The cycle of "birth" and "death" of vegetation that is so crucial for human survival has had profound effects on religious beliefs. The deities supposedly responsible for the growth of crops are highly honored, and in some religions there is the figure of a dying god whose rebirth is connected with the earth seeming to come to life again in the spring. The biblical writers had to resist such symbols of the fertility cults of their neighbors, and we find little use of them to express belief in the one God of Israel. It is YHWH, not Ba`al, who provides grain and wine and oil (Hosea 2:8), but YHWH is not a conventional fertility god.

Just because of this, the image of the dying and resurrected seed in John 12:24-25 (part of the Gospel Reading for the Fifth Sunday In Lent in Year B and Tuesday of Holy Week, as well as for Holy Cross Day in the *Lutheran Book of Worship* lectionary) is remarkable. Belief in the resurrection is based on that of Jesus, but Jesus himself is never pictured as (to recall C. S. Lewis' term) a Corn-King in the New Testament. In fact, as Lewis points out, in the one place where we might expect such an idea to emerge, when Jesus takes bread and says, "This is my body," there is no hint of it. "It is almost," Lewis comments, "as if He didn't realize what He had said." (C. S. Lewis, *Miracles* [New York: Macmillan, 1947], pp. 116-119.)

Agriculture, in the sense of planting and harvesting of plants for food rather than simply collecting edible fruits, nuts, and roots, has been part of human culture for thousands of years.

What we know of the division of labor in hunter-gatherer societies that have survived to the present day suggests that women, engaged primarily in finding vegetation for food while males would have been engaged primarily in hunting, may have been the inventors of agriculture. I have made use of this possibility in the present story sermon. In order to give it something of a primitive air, without (I hope) making the people in the story sound stupid, I deliberately kept the vocabulary and sentence structure quite simple throughout.

Chapter Eleven

The Bread Of Heaven

Acts 1:1-11

"This could be kind of embarrassing!" she thought as she looked at the computer screen and read the text from Acts that she needed to preach some kind of homily on that evening:

"When he had said this, as they were watching, he was lifted up, and a cloud took him out of their sight."

Of course she'd read this story of the Ascension of Jesus many times before and had even preached on it. She'd been ordained for ten years now, but this time it was different.

Now she wasn't in a seminary library or in her study in a parish church. Instead, she was sitting at a messy desk in a biochemistry laboratory on the planet Mars, a laboratory that represented her day job. It was here that she analyzed samples of air and soil and water in order to provide data that would help in judging the progress of the massive project of terraforming the planet. The fact that she was also a pastor and could serve as a Christian chaplain for the scientists and engineers engaged in this project had been, she knew perfectly well, something of an afterthought. Pastoral care and preaching and theology were hardly the highest priorities for the Extraterrestrial Development Agency of the U.N. It was fortunate that they'd been interested in providing any religious leadership at all.

And now one of the members of the small ecumenical congregation had brightly pointed out a few days ago that it would soon be the Feast of the Ascension, and that it would be nice to have a service in the evening. She hadn't bothered to tell him that since they were now on another planet with a different orbital period and rotation rate, it was completely artificial to say that this was the fortieth day after Easter. But you didn't want to discourage people who have a desire to worship, and she agreed. So here she was at her lunch hour, looking over the texts and realizing how archaic they seemed in this context.

"He was lifted up" — just as the old paintings of the Ascension showed it — Jesus floating up to the sky. "And a cloud took him out of their sight" — as if heaven were just a few kilometers above the earth, hidden behind some bits of water vapor! And here they were on Mars, able to go out and see the earth as a bright star 100 million kilometers distant. The big galaxy in Andromeda, three million light years away, was easily visible through the thin Martian atmosphere. How did Jesus lifting up from the earth to be "seated at the right hand of the Father" fit into *that* picture?

Oh, of course, the cloud is a symbol of the presence of God. Jesus didn't really rise up like a balloon to sit down on a throne somewhere out in space. It wasn't that her faith depended on the literal truth of any of those pictures — but how were you supposed to talk about it? What did this story of the Ascension really have that meant anything today when people were traveling through a much vaster universe than those writers of the Bible were aware of?

Well, maybe there were some other texts in the Bible that would be more helpful than the one from Acts. She said "Search: ascend" and a list of verses appeared on the screen. Hmm, this one from Ephesians 4 is interesting. "He who descended is the same one who ascended far above all the heavens, so that he might fill all things." That's a little better — Christ being present throughout the universe, but it's still not very easy to picture. After all, we're talking about Jesus, the one who showed the disciples the marks of the nails, and if we believe that the body that hung on the cross was really raised from the dead, then somehow we have to talk about the presence of that body.

That's the real problem — where's the body? Where is Jesus? He is not just an idea or a memory but an embodied person. I need to be able to say that in a way that makes sense here and now, 2251 A.D. on Mars. But how?

She didn't get much beyond that and soon had to go back to work in the lab, trying to see how well some of the microorganisms they'd introduced were surviving the frigid Martian climate. And when the small group of Christians gathered that evening, she didn't feel that she had anything very profound to say. The room was dark when they entered, and the view through the thick window, with sharp unwinking stars looking down on the harsh orange desert, reminded them all that they were no longer on the home planet. One of Mars' tiny moons could be seen moving across the sky. The homily said little about the Ascension itself and nothing about the body, and spoke instead about the promise of the Spirit. It was, the homilist felt, pretty feeble.

But now it was time for the meal with its familiar words. "The Lord be with you." "And also with you." Words that carried their own meaning, even if you weren't thinking about every one of them, even if you didn't understand all of them. "Heaven and earth are full of your glory" — and at that a couple of people glanced at the window, thinking of the stark landscape and starscape.

Then the most familiar words of all — "Our Lord Jesus Christ took bread" — she raised the loaf — "Take, eat: This is my Body" — and stopped. It was one of those moments that seems like hours though the clock ticks only once. "*This* is my body which is given for you. You need not understand the fullness of my new and unending life, a life that you, too, will share. It is indeed far above all heavens and fills all things. 'A little while, and you will no longer see me' and 'I am with you always, to the end of the age.' Because I fill all things, there is no place where you cannot take bread and wine and say, 'This is my Body, this is my Blood of the New Covenant.' "

"Do not worry about where I am when you are not there. Be assured that I am here for you in this action, wherever you may be."

The moment passed, and somehow she was able to end the prayer. And as each of the members of the congregation came forward she broke a piece from the loaf, placed it in the person's hand, and said, "The Body of Christ, the bread of heaven."

Comment

The story of the Ascension of Christ in the text from Acts has often been highlighted as one of the most obvious instances of a mythological worldview in the Bible. Certainly it seems to make

67

use of an obsolete "three decker" picture of the universe that is impossible to reconcile with modern understandings of the universe. Attempts to harmonize this picture with modern views are not helpful. The story does, however, raise an important question for Christians: If Jesus is indeed risen, where is he? Or more to the point, where does he encounter us?

One way in which he promises to be present for us is in the breaking of bread: "This is my body." At the time of the Reformation, debates about the Eucharist drew in the topic of the Ascension. "If," one line of argument went, "Christ did ascend into heaven 'and is seated at the right hand of the Father' then his body can't be present on earth. Thus he can't be present in a bodily fashion in the Eucharist." Luther's response to this was to reverse the argument. Since the body and blood of Christ *are* present in the Eucharist, his ascension and session must be understood in some way that is compatible with this presence. He argued that God's "right hand" means God's effective power and thus that "the right hand of God is everywhere." ("Confession concerning Christ's Supper" in *Luther's Works*, Volume 37 [Philadelphia: Muhlenberg, 1961], p. 214.) This means that the divine-human Christ is present to the entire universe, as passages like the one quoted in the sermon from Ephesians 4:10 suggest.

This sermon suggests the same line of argument. While thinking about how Christ can indeed be present to the whole universe is a legitimate issue for science-theology dialogue, we are to begin with the fact that he does promise to be present *for us* in the Eucharist. This will be as true for humans on Mars in the twenty-third century as for those in Europe in the sixteenth. That is where we can begin our theological reflection.

John 16:16 and Matthew 28:20 are quoted near the end of the sermon, together with some phrases from the Communion liturgy in *The Book of Common Prayer*. The phrase "The Body of Christ, the bread of heaven" (together with "The Blood of Christ, the cup of salvation") is part of one of the distribution formulae suggested there.

Chapter Twelve

I Am Christ's Body

1 Corinthians 12:12-31a

Years ago, *Reader's Digest* had a series of articles about a man named Joe and his wife, Jane. They were unusual because they had titles like "I Am Joe's Heart" and "I Am Jane's Womb," and were told in the first person by those parts of the body. Those different organs would tell about what they did, why they were important for our health, what we could do to take better care of them, and so forth. Very educational.

But I'm afraid that a lot of the story never got told. There were some unpleasant episodes that got hushed up. That's not too surprising. You know how it is in your family when people have a quarrel — you usually don't want to go out and tell everyone about it. When there are disagreements among members of our church, we don't want everybody in the world to know it. Well, there was the same kind of problem with the body. The sad fact is that the different parts of the body weren't really getting along well with one another. They just couldn't seem to get together.

Oh, they were *together* — they had to be, of course. They all lived in the same skin. They were like members of a family who live in the same house but are always disagreeing, or residents of a town who get together once a month at the school board meeting or city council to argue. The different parts of the body lived together, and every once in awhile they'd get together to quarrel.

A lot of the organs thought that they were the most important, and that all the rest of them ought to recognize that. The heart would say, "None of the rest of you could get along for a minute without me. I do the most important work, and if things don't get done the right way — which is my way — then I may just shut off the blood for the rest of you. No more free ride." And, of course, the heart *was* the biggest giver in the body, so nobody wanted to offend him. And the brain — she would say, "Thinking is what a body is really for. I don't have time to be worrying about the problems the rest of you have. I've got important thoughts to think." And she thought to herself how much nicer it would be if the body were all brain. Of course, then she'd have some problems like figuring out how to get oxygen and a few other things that brains need, but she wouldn't have to associate with embarrassing things like kidneys and toes!

Or the skin — that's what everyone *sees*. It's essential protection that the body needs to stay alive, and also wonderful decoration. A body has to keep up appearances, so the skin should get everything it wants, shouldn't it?

When the parts of the body got together, one of their favorite activities was bad-mouthing the mouth. "We just keep on feeding it, and all it does is talk." The mouth had plenty to say about that but they were tired of hearing all his speeches. Nobody likes a smart mouth after a while.

There were other parts of the body who were maybe too humble — run of the mill things like elbows and fingernails and the gall bladder. They thought that they weren't important at all because they didn't do any of the really essential jobs and nobody admired them. People put pretty pictures of hearts on things to say, "I love you." Have you ever seen a valentine with a picture of an elbow on it?

And then there were parts of the body that didn't seem to do anything at all, that were just kind of hidden away and inactive — useless things like the appendix and earlobes. The other parts of the body didn't know what they were good for and thought that they were just hangers-on. Sometimes, though, there would be a flare-up of appendicitis and or something like that, and trouble for the whole body.

So that's the way a lot of their discussions went, with complaints and cries. "I'm tired of doing all the work. I'm going to quit." "I'm tired of this body — I'm going to get transplanted." "I can do all right on my own — I don't need to be part of a body." (The feet were going to leave and get jobs as place-kickers in the National Football League.) Some said, "Everybody should be like me," and some cried, "I'm not good for anything," while others just wished that someone would notice the contributions that they made.

But then one day, the brain had something new to tell them. "I just realized something," she said. "We are most ourselves when we are closest together." Brains sometimes make puzzling remarks: They are quite smart and say things that are difficult to understand. So the other parts of the body just said, "Do you want to explain that?"

"Okay," said the brain. "We are most ourselves when we're closest to one another. Or in other words, we're the most individual when we're part of a community. I know it sounds strange — that's why I never thought of it before, as smart as I am." She paused for a moment as the others waited impatiently, then went on.

"Look. Each one of us has a specific thing that we're supposed to do and can do well. Take the heart for example. He pumps blood. As long as he works at that, he's a good heart. He doesn't have to digest food, or walk, or even look pretty. If he had to do those things he wouldn't be able to concentrate on pumping blood, and wouldn't be a very good heart."

"But," the stomach, who was usually argumentative, broke in, "the heart wouldn't last very long if it weren't for me getting the food and the lungs breathing and all those things."

"Exactly," said the brain. "It's when each one of us is doing what we're good at, what we're made for, that all the others are also what *they* are distinctively meant to be. The skin is supposed to look good. (Yes, I know, you really do.) But without the rest of us you'd be just an empty sack.

"And those obscure parts, those organs that don't seem to be good for anything. (I'm sorry they're not here now. Maybe they'd attend more regularly if they were made to feel more like parts of the body.) How do we know how important they are? Remember, we used to think that the pituitary gland was useless. Then we figured out that the whole body never would have grown up without it."

"I get it," said the heart. "You're saying that we're all important to one another because we're specialized. Each of us has got something that only he or she can do."

"That's part of it," said the brain. "But it's more than just that. Take the elbow. Apart from the rest of the body, it would just be some funny-shaped piece of bone. (No offense of course!) But when it's together with all the proper muscles and blood vessels and so on, you see how marvelously made it is for its job. When it's together with all the other parts, you say, "Wow! That's what an elbow *really* is."

And the other parts of the body nodded as if a light had been turned on for them. "That's right. We're most ourselves when we work together."

Then the gall bladder (who was never expected to say anything intelligent) spoke up rather hesitantly. "Yes — when we're together. But that means more than just being thrown together any which way. We have to be in the right places and in the right relationships with one another. When we are, we're more than just a collection of pieces. We're — a body. Somehow, that's more than an assembly of organs that happen to be held together. It's something higher. I wonder if that means that our creator never really meant for us to be separate."

"That's probably true," said the brain thoughtfully. (Of course, the brain said everything thoughtfully.) We must have been meant to be brought together, to become something greater than each one of us individually. We were meant from the beginning to be parts of the body."

"Yes," said the heart, "but don't forget what you said to begin with. In becoming a body, in going beyond our apartness and not trying to manage completely on our own, we become most clearly individual. When we are parts of the body, we are most fully everything we were meant to be as individuals."

For just as the body is one and has many members, and all the members of the body, though many, are one body, so it is with Christ ... Now you are the body of Christ and individually members of it.
— 1 Corinthians 12:12, 27

72

Comment

The *Reader's Digest* articles by J. D. Ratcliff were collected in *I Am Joe's Body* (New York: Berkley, 1975). This provides some details for working out Paul's analogy — which is stronger than a mere literary illustration — of the church as the body of Christ. Because different organs have different properties, the whole body can function effectively. On the other hand, because they are parts of one body, they can be distinctively different.

Teilhard de Chardin saw a connection between what happened in the course of evolution when individual cells came together to form more complex organisms and the coming together of individual persons to form the body of which Christ is the head, and he suggested that the church is the next stage of evolution. "Union," Teilhard said, "Creates ... differentiates ... [and] *personalizes.*" (Pierre Teilhard de Chardin, *Activation of Energy* [New York: Harcourt Brace Jovanovich, 1970], pp. 115-116.) We see the creative effect of union when a person who may have seemed bland and undistinguished suddenly "comes alive" in a gathering of his or her family or close friends. We have already emphasized the differentiating effect of union, and Teilhard's final point is we become most fully personal when we are in fellowship with other people.

Chapter Thirteen

The Signal

Ephesians 3:7-12

"What do you make of those references to their religious beliefs?" asked Habib, who was piloting the shuttle. It was a question that all five of the astronauts from earth had thought about. They had been immersed in the information from the scanty communications between earth and the Aquilans. (Everybody referred to the extraterrestrials by the name of the constellation in which their star was located. That star itself had had only a catalogue number when earth received its first communications from them.) But religious questions hardly had the top priority in the preparations for First Contact. Everyone assumed that an advanced technological civilization wouldn't insist upon any religious prejudices or taboos — although, as actual contact approached, all sort of worries, sensible or not, had begun to surface.

"There are a lot of features of their culture that we should have found out about more," said Nolumba, the anthropologist. "I understand why we're doing it this way," she said. "With a lag of over 100 years for electromagnetic signals and the hyperdrive just coming on line, we didn't have the patience to get to know them better before direct contact. They initiated communications with us after picking up our old radio and television transmissions, so we know they wanted us to be in touch with them. But without an adequate understanding of their cultures, we could be walking into trouble."

"We know enough," said Chen. As the ambassador who was officially in charge of the mission, he felt that he had to be positive. "We've learned over the past three centuries how much all the major religions on earth are alike. The Aquilans seem to have a general belief in a single deity and a system of morality that's a lot like those of earth's major religions. It's all pretty standard. Of course, when it comes to details we'll probably learn some things that will surprise people like you who study cultures."

"I don't know that there's really that much agreement even on earth," said Ibanez. "Buddhists don't believe in a God in the way that Muslims do, and theoretical morality doesn't always show itself in real life. The morality of European Christians sounded fine in theory, but how did it actually work out in practice with their colonialism and missionaries in America and Africa and Asia?"

The medical doctor had been shaking his head and now spoke up. "I'll be surprised if their religion has any real significance at all for them by this time. They're an advanced civilization with a science as good as ours, even if they don't have the hyperdrive yet. They won't take the idea of gods and miracles and demons seriously. Just like earth — some people may pay lip service to our myths, but those who are educated don't actually think of them as being true."

Habib laughed. "Clarke, I think you're the only full-blown atheist here. But now let's quiet down. I've got to land this thing, and I'm sure that the Aquilans would be more offended by my setting it down on top of the waiting crowd than by any religious differences."

* * * * *

The Terrestrials had known what the Aquilans would look like, but it still took some getting used to. A linkage between bipedalism and intelligence had seemed so obvious in the evolution of *homo sapiens* that people had come to think of it as a foregone conclusion. "So much for theory," thought Nolumba as she looked at the three Aquilans in the bus-like conveyance that was taking them from the landing site to their city. Their shapes reminded her of nothing so much as large dogs, although the digits on all four extremities seemed to function as well or better than human fingers. Sophisticated as the earthlings thought they were in the ways of the cosmos, it was hard not to smile at what seemed like talking Great Danes.

"I sure wish that spacesuits weren't necessary," whispered Habib. They gave a sense of distance that made it hard to feel that they were really in contact with the other beings. But while the

76

Aquilans were oxygen breathers, all kinds of microorganisms could cause havoc in earth systems.

Radio and television contacts had enabled earthlings to get a fair working knowledge of the major Aquilan language, but there was still some awkwardness in the bus. How do you carry on a conversation with an alien that you've just met? (But, of course, the earthlings were really the aliens here!) "Nice weather"? "How's your mom"? The diplomat Chen, however, wasn't having any problem. He was chatting with the Aquilans, trying skillfully to get all the information he could.

Suddenly, one of their hosts broke off the conversation and pointed out a window. "We are coming to the city," it said. "We will go first to the Temple." The earthlings looked at one another. Perhaps religion wasn't a secondary concern after all.

The buildings of the city were low and rectangular — an efficient shape if you didn't have to worry about retaining air. Analysis of transmissions from Aquila had led them to believe that there were extensive underground facilities. The bus stopped in front of one building that didn't seem to differ much from the others. The embassy from earth was escorted inside, its members having to stoop to get through the low door.

They entered a large room — and stopped in amazement. At the front of the room was a large cross.

"What the...!" gasped Ibanez. The others just stared — except for Clarke. The doctor motioned the others forward impatiently. "It's a simple geometric figure," he said. "It could mean anything."

"Don't look as if you're offended," said Chen in a low voice. He got his bewildered group seated on one of the benches that had been provided for them. One of their hosts, whose dress somehow set him off from the others, walked to the front of the room and faced the earthlings. "Greetings," it said, "In the name of Jesus Christ."

The earthlings sat in stunned silence, hearing little of what seemed to be a prayer and a welcoming speech. When it was clear that some response was called for, Chen stumbled out some formalities. But when two of the Aquilans approached them, Habib blurted out, "Jesus Christ? How have you heard of him?"

"Why, from your electromagnetic transmissions," said the Aquilan. "We had had many ideas about the meaning of the world, and some of our cultures had a belief in a single God, but we first heard about Jesus from your Bishop Sheen."

"Our who?" asked Clarke. But Nolumba had pulled a computer from her pocket and punched the name in.

"Fulton Sheen. Roman Catholic bishop, United States of North America, mid-twentieth century. First religious program on national television, CE 1952."

"1952!" exclaimed Ibanez. "That must have been right at the beginning of commercial television."

"Yes, yes," said the Aquilan. "It was one of the earliest video transmissions that we detected." He moved to a panel and manipulated some equipment to bring a plasma screen to life. There was some grainy footage of a human in some strange old-fashioned clothing standing on a stage and talking. The Aquilan made a few adjustments and they heard a voice speaking in archaic English.

"You see?" said their host. He went on as the screen darkened. "We first heard about Jesus in that way. Later we were able to find out more from transmissions with your Billy Graham and other humans. We were puzzled by much of what they said, but it seemed interesting. As we received more transmissions and were able to learn more about Jesus, many of our people began to believe that this gave us a deeper knowledge of God than we had had before. The idea that God would come to live in our universe and share the death of creatures so that they could share God's life was one that we had never heard of before."

"But that's an earth religion," said Habib. "What made you think...?"

"Yes, yes, of course. We argued quite a lot about that. Was this story of Jesus only for the people of your planet? Some of us thought so. But others believed that if the story really was true then it couldn't be limited to one planetary system. They suggested that our reception of your signals was a way that God used to tell the story to us. What decided the question for most of us was when we received a transmission in which one of your people read from something that was called a letter to the Ephesians."

Now the Aquilan's tone of voice changed as he began to quote from memory words in an old English like that of Bishop Sheen:

Although I am the very least of all the saints, this grace was given to me to bring to the Gentiles the news of the boundless riches of Christ, and to make everyone see what is the plan of the mystery hidden for ages in God who created all things; so that through the church the wisdom of God in its rich variety might now be made known to the rulers and authorities in the heavenly places. This was in accordance with the eternal purpose that he has carried out in Christ Jesus our Lord, in whom we have access to God in boldness and confidence through faith in him. — Ephesians 3:8-12

Comment

In his novel, *Contact* (New York: Simon & Schuster, 1985), Carl Sagan made dramatic use of the idea that extraterrestrials would retransmit to earth the first terrestrial broadcasts they received as a way of showing that they were aware of us. In the movie, starring Jodie Foster, which was based on this novel, the scene in which the signal picked up by radio astronomers is resolved into a video image of Adolf Hitler at first seems an absurdity, but it quickly becomes quite reasonable. One of the first television broadcasts was, in fact, of the opening of the 1936 Berlin Olympics by the German dictator. Traveling outward at the speed of light, these signals could be picked up by another technological civilization.

I have stretched things a bit in order to make use of a similar idea here. Fulton Sheen's program "Life is Worth Living" was the first nationwide religious program on television, but it didn't go on the air until a few years after the beginning of commercial television in the United States. Religious programs with Billy Graham and other speakers (some of whom, to be frank, I would just as soon extraterrestrials *wouldn't* pick up) soon followed. I did not try to tie the story to any specific historical broadcast, but made use of the idea in a quite general way.

The reference in the Ephesians text to the making known of God's wisdom "to the rulers and authorities [*tais archais kai tais exousiais* — in the King James Version, 'the principalities and powers'] in the heavenly places" in its original setting refers to the idea that it must be proclaimed to angelic beings. But how would it sound to extraterrestrials? Perhaps with appropriate demythologizing we should see this as a call to cosmic mission — without the kind of exploitation to which Ibanez refers in the story.

Chapter Fourteen

Superhero: Sort Of A Sequel

Hebrews 12:1-2

The city was dark. At night the skies and streets were black, as criminals worked almost anywhere they pleased. No one was safe from muggers, rapists, or junkies trying to steal a few dollars for their next fix. Gangs of the unemployed and unemployable roamed the streets and alleys, fighting each other and beating people to death to relieve the boredom of their lives. Shadows were everywhere.

Things used to be good. Older citizens remembered when they could go to a movie downtown in the evening, walk the well-lighted streets, or sit on a bench in the park without fearing for their lives. Now you'd have to be crazy to do anything like that. Most people had forgotten about being either safe or happy, and just assumed that life had to be rotten.

Even during the day the city was dark. That was partly because of the air pollution that no one tried to control, pollution that turned the skies gray and kept the sun from penetrating into the canyons of the city even at noontime. But the sense of darkness also came from the well-known fact that the city was run by crooks — crooks in the mayor's office, the police force, and leaders of businesses and labor unions. No one was free from them.

But few of the citizens had seen, or even knew about, the one who was at the top of the heap and bossed all this crime. He was the one who sat in his comfortable office and laughed at the television news reports about earnest citizens' groups and reforming political candidates who wanted to do something about crime and corruption. They talked solemnly about "studying" the drug problem, "cracking down" on pornography and prostitution or "demanding" clean air. But of course nothing ever came of their efforts.

It was all quite funny, especially if you were the Jester. Naturally, the Jester enjoyed his control of the city, but it especially appealed to his rather special sense of humor to play with these naive little people who were trying to do something about the darkness. Let an investigation by a citizens' group or some law enforcement program move along to the point where people were just thinking that they might accomplish something — and then some witnesses would be intimidated or a well-planned scandal would involve one of the reformers, and the whole thing would fall apart. Then the Jester would lean back in his chair and laugh at the naive do-gooders who didn't know what had hit them.

He had refined this business of controlling things by humiliating his opponents to a fine art. It gave the Jester a lot of pleasure, so that he hardly ever needed to shoot people himself anymore to have fun.

Of course, there were also those who wanted to get tough with crime. Some of them formed vigilante groups or tried to play superhero. Occasionally, they would arrest or kill a few criminals, and sometimes they got arrested or killed themselves. It wasn't always easy to tell the difference between the superheroes and the criminals, and that provided more laughs for the Jester.

Late one evening, a small-time hood was holding a gun on a terrified old man on a deserted side street. He was thumbing through the contents of the old man's wallet with his other hand. Quietly, a man in a conservative gray suit stepped from the shadows and said, "You shouldn't be doing that. Give his money back to him."

The mugger glanced at the newcomer in a puzzled way. "Hey — you crazy? You trying to be funny? Get outta here and maybe you won't get hurt!"

"Trying to be funny? I guess you could say that. Perhaps, I should give you my business card," and he held out a small piece of white cardboard.

In that situation, the gesture was so strange that the mugger was at a loss for a second, and in confusion juggled the gun and wallet as he tried to get a free hand to take the card. Suddenly both gun and wallet were in the stranger's hands. The gun went sailing into the darkness of the alley and the wallet was back in the old man's pocket.

"What are you doing?" yelled the stunned robber. "Who do you think you are — Batman?"

"Not at all. Just plain, 'Man,' will do, and please pass the word to your boss that from now on the joke is on him." He turned and walked away. The would-be mugger picked up the card from the pavement. On it there was a picture of a man hanging from a gallows and the words, "Enthronements our specialty: Call 1-800-564-6316."

When the Jester heard about this, he wasn't amused. "Some smart aleck imitator" he said, looking at the card with the hanged man on it. "What kind of sicko humor is this supposed to be? He's trying to make me look stupid. Get rid of him," he said to his henchmen who were standing around. "Nobody jests with the Jester."

But it's hard to get rid of someone whose appearances are always unexpected, and who never does what you anticipate. When Man showed up during a crime in progress, preposterous things happened. The criminals were confused and the intended victims usually left with more money than they'd started with. He always left his card with the gallows and the phone number, 1-800-564-6316.

Of course, the newspapers and television stations wanted pictures and interviews, but they didn't have much luck. Some people thought he must be another criminal trying to muscle in on the Jester's territory, but the MO didn't really fit. The only people who were getting hurt were criminals and dishonest officials.

When the drug dealers brought their briefcases of $100 bills to the Jester's office one day, they turned out to be full of Monopoly money. They didn't laugh, and they didn't feel any better when they found that all the cocaine that they'd smuggled in was high-grade confectioner's sugar. The next day, all the streetwalkers on Fifth Avenue were handing out Bible Society tracts. And, somehow, foul-smelling sludge was getting into the hot tubs of corporate officials who'd been dumping waste into the river.

The Jester sat fuming in his plush office. There was nothing funny about this. Now *he* was the joke. He was deep in thought, and only gradually realized that someone was standing there. "I thought it was time we met," said the man in the gray suit. "My card." And he held out the picture of the gallows.

"You're pushing your luck," the Jester said. "What are you after? Revenge for something? Want to be a hero and have the women fall into your arms? Or do you just want a cut of the take?"

"No, nothing as complicated as that," said Man. "It's just that life is supposed to be good for everybody. There's something wrong when a few people enjoy it at the expense of everyone else."

"So, it's just another moral crusade," sneered the man behind the desk. "Next thing I know you'll be telling me what God wants me to do! Look — everyone's a crook. Everybody's looking out for Number One. I'm just better at it than they are. You're going to persuade me to give up my advantage by becoming a good citizen? Don't make me laugh!"

"I wish I could," said the other. "Of course, you're right — they all are crooked. Everyone has a lot of meanness and selfishness inside. But the joke, you see, is that I love them anyway. And the real knee-slapper — wait for it! — The real joke is that I even love you!"

Suddenly, a gun was in the Jester's hand. "The joke's gone far enough," he snarled, and a sadistic smile crossed his face. "Have you ever traded jokes with the devil?" he asked softly, and pulled the trigger. But all that came out was a little flag with the word "BANG" printed on it. Man said, "So long — it's been fun," and slipped out.

Of course they got him eventually. He was captured and they put some charges together, bribed a jury to convict him, and sentenced him to be hanged. While the drug dealers and murderers were getting off with slaps on the wrist, his sentence was carried out quickly. And when the body had been cut down, the Jester said, "That's the end of that wise guy."

The Jester usually guessed right, but this time he was way off.

They didn't have to wait too long for the punch line. When they got the cheap wooden coffin out to the graveyard, to the run-down section where the paupers were buried, one of the grave-diggers said, "This coffin's too light. Somebody musta' made a mistake. Let's don't waste our time." So they pried the lid off the coffin and found it empty — or almost empty. In it there was a card with a picture of a man hanging from the gallows and the words, "Enthronements our specialty: Call 1-800-JOH-N316."

Comment

Many films of the superhero genre are pretty forgettable. The 1989 *Batman* with Michael Keaton as Batman and Jack Nicholson as the Joker was something of an exception. Unlike characters with superhuman powers such as Superman, Batman is genuinely human, albeit with plenty of technological gadgetry at his disposal. Keaton was able to make him more than just a one-dimensional fighter for goodness, and Nicholson's manic performance in a similar way fleshed out the villain.

This sermon was preached in the summer in which that film was released. This is always something of a risk: Even if a film (or television program or book) has received a lot of public attention, there may be many members in any given congregation who know nothing about it. Sometimes, though, that is a risk one takes in order to try to address the gospel to popular culture. I've modified that earlier version of this story sermon a little so that it is not so heavily dependent on *Batman*. Those who have seen that movie, however, will recognize a number of the references.

The phone number in the sermon is probably too subtle for oral delivery. But JOHN is, in fact, 5646 on a normal touchtone phone, and spelling out JOH-N316 at first would give too much away.

The suggested text is part of the Second Lesson, Hebrews 11:29—12:2, for Proper 15 in Year C of the Revised Common Lectionary. The earlier part of the reading refers to some of the "superheroes" of Israel's story, but I had in mind especially the statement in 12:2 about Jesus who "endured the cross, disregarding [RSV "despising"] its shame." This suggests a note of defiance of the powers of evil.

Essay One

Real Faith And Fictional Worlds

(An edited version of this essay was published as "Religion in Science Fiction" in Forum Letter 27.5, 1998. The original — though slightly corrected — version is used here by permission.)

What will be the status of religion in the twenty-fourth century? With all the proliferation and intermingling of faiths today, it may be surprising that the answer will be so simple. Some extraterrestrials will have one religion that pervades their culture and is common to their entire species. Klingons have a warrior religion much like that of the old Norse, and at least the outward aspects of Bajoran piety look like Hinduism. And *homo sapiens*? Well, we've outgrown all that. We've conquered poverty and bigotry, and need no religion.

J. B. Phillips pointed out in his 1961 book, *Your God is too Small*, that writers can give an impression of the irrelevance of God and religion simply by presenting fiction in which they play no role. Science fiction, which at that time was only a fringe area of literature and film, can today serve as a clear example of Phillips' argument. The *Star Trek* sagas, from which my opening examples are taken, might be Exhibit A.

Before anyone shies away from this as a diatribe against science fiction, let me say that I've paid my dues in that club. In junior high and high school, I spent vast amounts of time reading and re-reading Heinlein, Asimov, Van Vogt, and other major and minor sci-fi authors, raced to see the classic, *Forbidden Planet*, in its first run, and still watch *Star Trek* spin-offs and some of the profusion of today's good and bad sci-fi films. As with any genre, many science fiction novels and films are mediocre. But at its best, the medium can give penetrating insight into the possibilities for science and technology and their impacts on individuals and cultures. Having lived through the time before Sputnik and Apollo when the idea of space travel was ridiculed, I have little patience with those who look down their noses at futuristic fiction.

Star Trek certainly has to be given a lot of the credit for mainstreaming science fiction. Some episodes of the original series and *Star Trek: Next Generation* (but fewer, I think, of the later series) involve themes which raise basically religious issues. There is, however, a clear avoidance of any human religious belief or practice — other than the politically correct Native American spirituality of Chakotay in *Voyager*. We don't have to look very far for the source of this: Joel Engel's biography of *Star Trek* creator, Gene Roddenberry, makes clear his hostility to religion and belief that humanity will be better off without it. (Cf. pp. 246-247: "At the Episcopal marriage of *Next Generation* star, Jonathan Frakes, Roddenberry was so offended by the liturgy that he very nearly left before the I-do's. 'He was going nuts,' Rick Berman says.")

There is another feature of *Star Trek* which, I suggest, has some connection with this neglect of the religious dimension: Human culture in *Star Trek* seems, in the last analysis, to be rather boring. In fact, that culture seems to have little content other than the ongoing exploration of the galaxy. The blandness of human society is a marked contrast to those of the Klingons and Bajorans, whose religions are integral parts of their cultures. Perhaps humanity has outgrown the internecine struggles that mark these other cultures, but the result seems a bit like naive versions of Christian eschatology in which eternity is spent sitting on clouds playing harps.

And science fiction can also express overt hostility to Christianity through the same process of creating an imaginary *reductio ad absurdum* of the faith. Robert Heinlein's 1984 novel, *Job: A Comedy of Justice*, is a good illustration. (The later Heinlein, especially when unable to keep his literary pants zipped, is something of an embarrassment to many of his fans of the '40s and '50s.)

Having pronounced judgment on science fiction in good law-gospel fashion, I hasten to note the good news. Religion, and specifically Christianity, does not have to be ignored or ridiculed in this genre. Science fiction makes possible new and provocative explorations of ultimate concerns, even if religion is not an explicit theme. Some technophiles got upset about the climactic battle in *Star Wars* in which Luke turns off his targeting computer and lets himself be guided by The Force. This is part of the rather vague eastern mysticism that becomes more explicit in the later films of the trilogy. Though it is not Christianity, it is not explicitly hostile to it.

Forbidden Planet, which I mentioned earlier, resonates with issues related to the doctrine of original sin: Humanity is threatened by its own version of "the mindless primitive" that destroyed the advanced beings of Altair IV in their hour of greatest technological achievement.

(The current film, *Sphere*, uses a similar idea, but not very successfully.) This is by no means just a retelling of Genesis 3 or Romans 5. In fact, the idea that evolved humanity must carry an inherited load of "monsters from the Id" poses some real challenges for an adequate Christian anthropology and the traditional idea that humanity was created with the ability not to sin. Besides its entertainment value, this film can serve as a focus for some thoughtful theological discussion in a congregation — once people get used to Leslie Nielsen in a serious role!

Science fiction can often function in that way, not by portraying a future in which Christianity is vindicated but by presenting thoughtful questions for traditional beliefs. The Christian protagonist of Arthur C. Clarke's short story "The Star," has to grapple with the discovery that the stellar explosion which was the Star of Bethlehem destroyed a magnificent civilization. In his whimsical fashion, Robert Sheckley in "The Battle" asked us to think about who the real victors will be if we use robotic armies to defeat the forces of darkness at Armageddon. And James Blish's, *A Case of Conscience*, makes interesting use of the Manichaean heresy as a plot device.

Positive presentations of Christianity in science fiction require some discipline. Scenarios of the future in which the author's version of orthodoxy triumphs may be just a mirror image of the areligious or antireligious themes that I have noted, and call for the same criticism. The novels and films representing what might be called "rapture fiction" come under this heading.

I think that C. S. Lewis' "space trilogy" escapes this criticism. In a sense what Lewis showed is that the "scientifiction" universe need not be devoid of spiritual realities, as it was in the work of writers like Wells and Stapledon. Human travel to Mars is less significant than the coming of Christ ["Maleldil"] to earth. And while the Tower of Babel built by science-based technology is toppled by a confusion of tongues in the final book, this is only one victory over evil and not the parousia.

Christianity can also play a central role in grittier plots. While angelic beings have a major role in Lewis' trilogy, *A Canticle for Leibowitz* by Walter M. Miller, Jr., made virtually no appeal to the overtly supernatural as it described the preservation of human culture by Christian monasticism after the nuclear Flame Deluge.

And where could we put Philip K. Dick in this picture? None of his work, which is sometimes brilliant and often confusing, could be considered an apologia for orthodox Christianity, but some of it (*The Divine Invasion*, for instance) is packed with bits of esoteric Judaeo-Christian lore. And one has to put in a good word for an author who could write a short story, "The Pre-Persons" (under twelve years old!), which enraged some of the abortion on demand crowd.

It might be nice to see the Eucharist celebrated on the next incarnation of the *Enterprise*, but don't hold your breath. Instead of hoping for a breakthrough like that, it might be profitable to think about ways in which the popularity of science fiction could be used for proclamation of, and reflection upon, the Christian message. I've already suggested that some films might serve as starters for worthwhile theological discussion. Preachers who feel more creative and serve congregations in which this is appropriate might think about developing a science fiction story sermon to put issues like cloning or extraterrestrial life in the context of the gospel. Try going where few have gone before.

For Further Reading
The fictional works I've referred to might be the best place to start. John Clute's *Science Fiction: The Illustrated Encyclopedia* (New York: Dorling Kindersley, 1995) gives an entertaining

overview of the field, while Robert Short's *The Gospel from Outer Space* (San Francisco: Harper & Row, 1982) focuses on the religious implications of some popular science fiction films. More specialized treatments are Joel Engel's *Gene Roddenberry: The Myth and the Man behind Star Trek* (New York: Hyperion, 1994) and David C. Downing's *Planets in Peril: A Critical Study of C. S. Lewis' Ransom Trilogy* (Amherst, Massachusetts: University of Massachusetts, 1992).

Essay Two

The Matrix And The Gospel

(This is a modified version of an essay that was originally published as part of *The Immediate Word* preaching resource for 18 May 2003. It is used here by permission. Copyright 2003 The Immediate Word/CSS Publishing. Address all correspondence regarding subscription requests to *The Immediate Word*, 517 South Main Street, P.O. Box 4503, Lima, Ohio 45802-4503, or call 800-241-4056, or visit <http://csspub.com>.)

The biggest religious news, at least of this month, may be the release of the long-anticipated sequel to the 1999 film *The Matrix*. *The Matrix Reloaded*, opened on May 15, 2003. Yes, it's still the Easter season and our Sunday readings continue to speak to us about what Jesus' resurrection means. Yes, the Shiite branch of Islam continues to be a powerful influence in post-war Iraq, and there are other important religious news items from throughout the world. But, many people will be more strongly influenced by the views about the nature of reality and the meaning of life in the second movie of the *Matrix* trilogy than by anything that they're hearing from representatives of organized religion — and that includes some of the people who will be sitting in the pews on Sunday.

The *Matrix* films aren't unique in using religious themes and influencing religious views. If you want something lighter, *Bruce Almighty* will debut on May 23. Here Bruce, played by Jim Carrey, will get to fill in for God (Morgan Freeman) and exercise divine power.

The task of the preacher is to communicate God's Word, law, and gospel, to people in the world in which they live. How are we to do that when their view of the world — and in fact ours, as well — is influenced in subtle and not-so-subtle ways by the religious views circulating in the media? These influences are not all bad or all good, and some care is needed in challenging some and using others to reinforce the Christian message.

Preachers want to present the gospel in an up-to-date way, which is one reason why we sometimes use popular films as illustrations. With all our desire to make preaching relevant to what's going on in the world and in the lives of our listeners, however, we have to make sure that we keep restating in clear ways the basic and distinctive teachings of the Christian faith. If we speak only in religious generalities about "God" and "love" then it may be hard for our hearers to distinguish what we're saying from things that they see and hear in popular media, things which may be in some tension with the gospel.

The *Matrix* films don't use explicit God language but the religious images are pretty obvious. One of the heroes is named Trinity and the last human city holding out against the machines that have enslaved the world is Zion. Keanu Reeves' character, Neo, who has been described in a number of reviews as a "Christ figure," often wears a black cassock-like garment that makes him look for all the world like a Roman Catholic or Anglican priest. There are plenty of other hints and allusions in the film — not all of them religious — and I won't spoil your fun in finding some for yourself.

But the religious content goes beyond symbolism. In the *Matrix* films, the world that most people experience is an illusion, the product of a tremendous computer program. They think that they're living in a society much like ours, but in reality they are stuck in pods and the energy they generate is being used by the machines that have taken over the world after a terrible war. Neo and others who have been freed from the world of the matrix are among the defenders of Zion, but they also have to go back into it in order to free others and fight the agents of the machines if humanity is ever to be saved from its enslavement.

The film is well done and I like it simply as science fiction. (Some of the techno-babble is, however, overdone.) There will be some objection to the violence in the martial arts and chase scenes, but it needs to be remembered that these things are taking place in a computer program rather than the real world. They are not blood and guts scenes, and are so well done that I often felt that I was watching elaborate choreography rather than a typical action film. (*The Matrix Reloaded* is rated R, but neither the violence nor the sexuality is of a type that would have made PG-13 impossible.)

But what about the religious message? From a Christian standpoint there are some questionable aspects. The idea that the world that we experience is not the true reality has a lot in common with the teachings of the Gnostics who were one of Christianity's main competitors in the early centuries. They held that the material world was the creation of an inferior deity (perhaps the God of the Old Testament), that our souls are trapped in the darkness of this material realm, and that the true God beyond the world sends the redeemer to enlighten people with the knowledge (*gnosis*) of their situation and thus free their souls and save them from the world. (The article "Gnosticism" by R. McL. Wilson in *The Westminster Dictionary of Christian Theology*, gives further information.)

This contrasts strongly with the Christian belief that the world is the good creation of the God who sent his Son into the world to save human beings from sin in their entire body-soul-spirit reality through faith in his death and resurrection. The Christian hope is the resurrection of the body in a transformed creation, not the salvation of some immaterial part of ourselves from the world.

To put the worst construction on it, the *Matrix* films might be seen as a kind of cyber-gnosticism, with Neo as an example of the gnostic redeemer myth rather than as a genuine Christ figure. It wouldn't be surprising to encounter something like this in a time when some versions of New-Age thought have a lot of resemblance to classical Gnosticism.

I don't think that it would be fair to the movie to leave it at that, however. The goal of those fighting the matrix isn't simply to get rid of the computerized illusion but also to free people from its bondage and give them full physical life. The *Matrix* films display no gnostic contempt for physical reality, as some of the scenes set in Zion make clear. We'll have to wait for the final third of the trilogy, scheduled for November, to see how it all turns out.

Meanwhile in our world, there are strong attempts to impose false realities upon people. Perhaps the most pervasive and widely accepted is our whole culture of consumerism that promotes the illusion that people can be happy and secure if they keep accumulating more and more possessions. Various kinds of political and religious propaganda provide other examples. And while Christianity teaches the saving role of faith rather than of knowledge, the latter is not insignificant. "My people are destroyed for lack of knowledge," God declares through Hosea (4:6), and Jesus says, "You will know the truth, and the truth will make you free" (John 8:32).

Bruce Almighty is not likely to fare very well in comparison with *The Matrix* and its sequel, at least as far as depth is concerned. Previews showing Bruce using his power to increase his girl friend's breast size and getting his dog to use the toilet aren't promising. But there is a hint that perhaps he's going to find out that there's more to being God than just throwing arbitrary miracles around. You'll have to see the movie when it opens if you want to pursue this. But I wouldn't ignore the film's impact just because it's unsophisticated. In the last generation (1977), George Burns as the deity in *Oh, God!* was pretty influential in presenting a warm-hearted, but rather simple-minded, deism.

How might proclamation this Sunday take some of these matters into account? In the lectionary texts for the Sixth Sunday Of Easter (Acts 10:44-48; Psalm 98; 1 John 5:1-6; and John 15:9-17), the most obvious single theme is that of love in the Second Lesson and the Gospel, and that would be a good thing to focus on.

The type of love, *agape*, of which these texts speak goes much deeper than "Can't we all just get along?" an idea that is encouraged (and, of course, is fine as far as it goes) by films like *Oh, God!* It is broader than the love connected with sexual attraction. (The love between Neo and Trinity is sexual but isn't limited to that. Their willingness to suffer and die for one another is an important part of the plot.) We know what genuine love is, and therefore can understand Jesus' commandment that we are to "love one another," because "I have loved you" (John 15:12). And that, in turn, is something that flows from the love of Father and Son (15:9-10).

Love, in fact, defines the character of God. "God is love (*agape*)" (1 John 4:16) was one of the texts for last Sunday and is the background of the reading from 1 John this week. It is, of course, a frequently quoted phrase but its full depth often isn't appreciated. The belief that God is love in God's own being ultimately requires something like a Trinitarian understanding of God. (See, for example, Eberhard Jüngel, *God as the Mystery of the World* [Eerdmans, 1983].) Thus any representation of God by a single actor, even one as good as Morgan Freeman, is bound to be inadequate. (On the other hand, some of the visual images of Neo, Trinity, and Morpheus together in *The Matrix Reloaded* are intriguing.)

Equally unsatisfactory is any representation of God simply as "the Almighty" without reference to God as love. To play off the idea of Bruce getting to be "almighty" for a day, a preacher might develop a story sermon in which someone has the opportunity to show the love of God in its fullness for a day. That could be introduced with a brief reference to the movie's theme, and hearers wouldn't even need to have seen the movie to get the point.

The fact that the love of God "spills over" from the inner life of God to the world is also important for understanding the goodness of creation over and against gnostic devaluations of it. John 3:16 is, of course, quoted even more often than "God is love." God's love for "the world" means love, first of all, for the world of human beings, a world that is estranged from God by sin but that is still God's good creation. And God's love is not limited to human beings. The thanksgiving at the beginning of Evening Prayer in *Lutheran Book of Worship* sings simply, "You love your whole creation." At this time of year many churches have a Sunday with some emphasis on care for creation (Earth Sunday, Rogationtide, Stewardship of Creation Sunday, Soil and Water Stewardship Sunday). This week's Psalm 98, in which all the earth is to "break forth into joyous song and sing praises" (v. 4) would fit in with such a theme.

Alternatively, a sermon might speak to some of the illusions that our culture tries to impose on us — "The one who dies with the most toys wins," "You've got to look out for Number One," "Power grows from the barrel of a gun," and so forth. These aren't as all-encompassing as the false world of the matrix, but are ubiquitous enough to make the analogy worth pursuing. The true reality, the hidden ground of all being, is the Love willing to die for the other. One of the questions that *The Matrix Reloaded* poses has to do with the nature of power and control. The Christ who saves by letting go (Philippians 2:5-11) is one biblical answer.

www.ingramcontent.com/pod-product-compliance
Lightning Source LLC
Chambersburg PA
CBHW072013170626
46813CB00005B/2141